The Three Stooges®

BED-BUGGED!

AND OTHER STORIES

PRESENTED BY C3 ENTERTAINMENT, INC.

PAPERCUTZ™

The Three Stooges®

GRAPHIC NOVELS AVAILABLE FROM PAPERCUTZ™

ALL-NEW! FULL-COLOR GRAPHIC NOVEL!
SEE THE NEW MOVIE!
The Three Stooges
PRESENTED BY C3 ENTERTAINMENT, INC.
BED-BUGGED!
PAPERCUTZ

THE THREE STOOGES #1 "BED-BUGGED"

The Best of THE THREE STOOGES Comicbooks
Volume 1
AS GOOD AS NEW, HUH?
BOING
Presented by C3 ENTERTAINMENT, INC.
by NORMAN MAURER & PETE ALVARADO
Introduction by JOAN MAURER
PAPERCUTZ

THE BEST OF THE THREE STOOGES COMICBOOKS: VOL. 1

BY NORM SAUNDERS
PETE ALVARADO
INTRO BY
JOAN MAURER

COMING SOON!

THE THREE STOOGES #2 "EBENEZER STOOGE"

THE THREE STOOGES #3 "CELL-BLOCKHEADS"

THREE STOOGES graphic novels are available in paperback and hardcover from booksellers everywhere. THE BEST OF THE THREE STOOGES COMICBOOKS is available in hardcover only from booksellers everywhere.

Or order from us: please add $4.00 for postage and handling for first book, add $1.00 for each additional book. THE THREE STOOGES #1 is $6.99 in paperback, and $10.99 in hardcover. THE BEST OF THE THREE STOOGES COMICBOOKS Vol. 1 is $19.99 each in hardcover only. Please make check payable to NBM Publishing. Send to: Papercutz 40 Exchange Place, Ste. 1308, New York, NY 10005 * 1-800-886-1223

www.papercutz.com

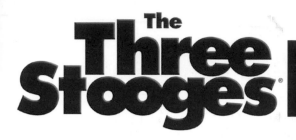

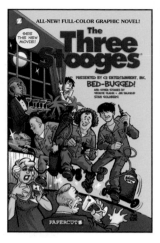

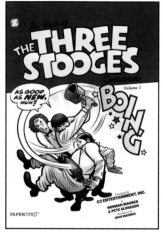

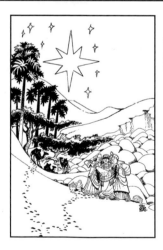

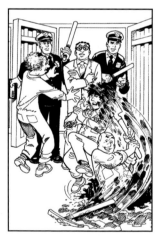

The Three Stooges ®

#1
BED-BUGGED!
AND OTHER STORIES

GEORGE GLADIR
JIM SALICRUP · WRITERS
STAN GOLDBERG · ARTIST
LAURIE E. SMITH · COLORIST

PAPERCUTZ ™
NEW YORK

The Three Stooges
#1 "Bed-Bugged!"

"Sumo of My Best Friends are Sumo!"
"Beating the Heat," "The 3 Buckaroos,"
"Shrinkage," "The Lost Survivors,"
"The Fame Game," "A Haunting We Will Go"
Script: George Gladir
Additional Dialogue: Jim Salicrup
Art: Stan Goldberg
Color: Laurie E. Smith
Lettering: Janice Chiang
"Bed-Bugged!"
Script: Jim Salicrup
Art: Stan Goldberg
Color: Laurie E. Smith
Lettering: Janice Chiang

Production by Nelson Design Group, LLC
Associate Editor – Michael Petranek
Jim Salicrup
Editor-in-Chief

ISBN: 978-1-59707-315-8 paperback edition
ISBN: 978-1-59707-316-5 hardcover edition

Printed in China
March 2012 by Asia One Printing LTD
13/F Asia One Tower
8 Fung Yip St., Chaiwan
Hong Kong

Distributed by Macmillan

First Printing

Meet the Stooges...
Moe

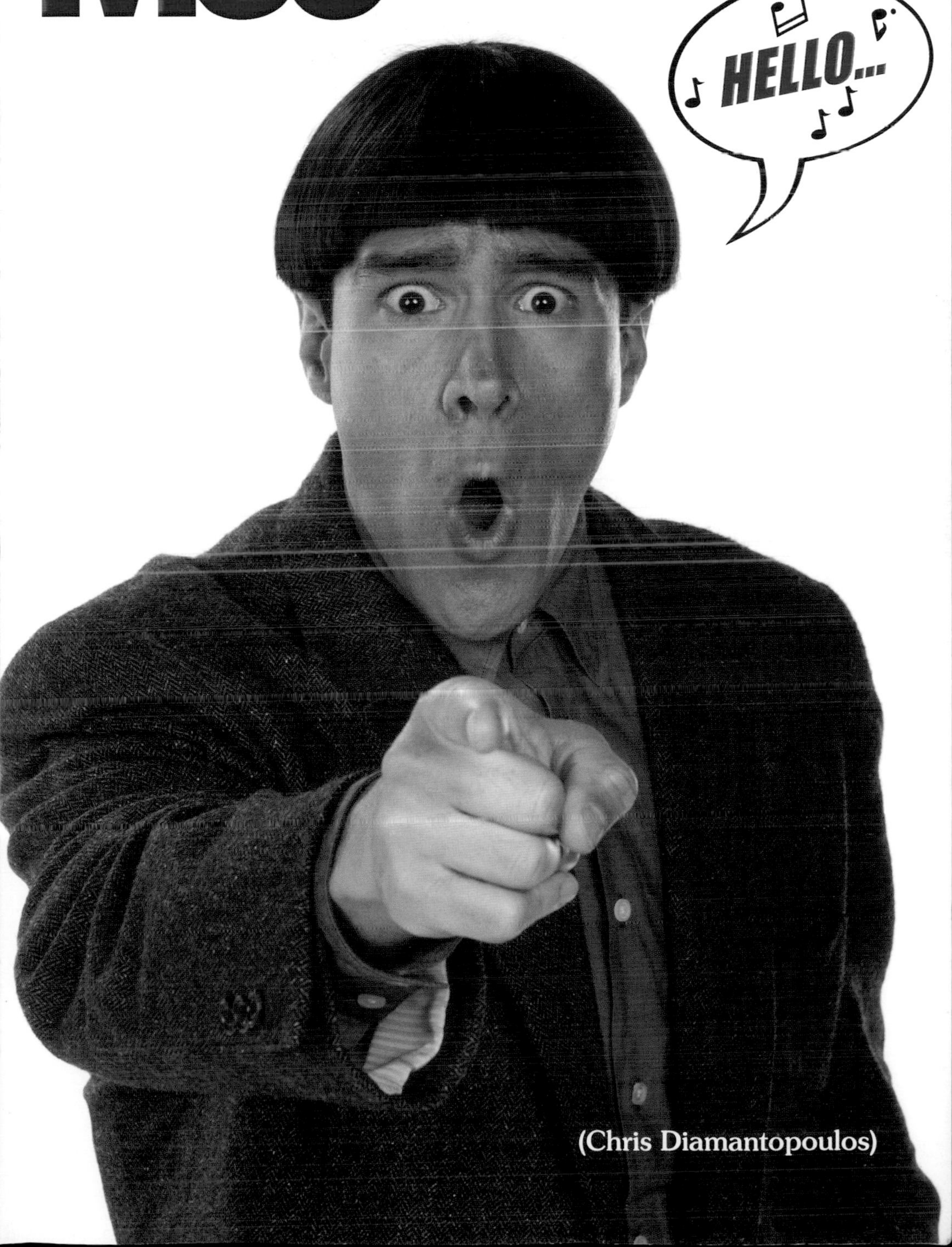
HELLO...

(Chris Diamantopoulos)

Larry

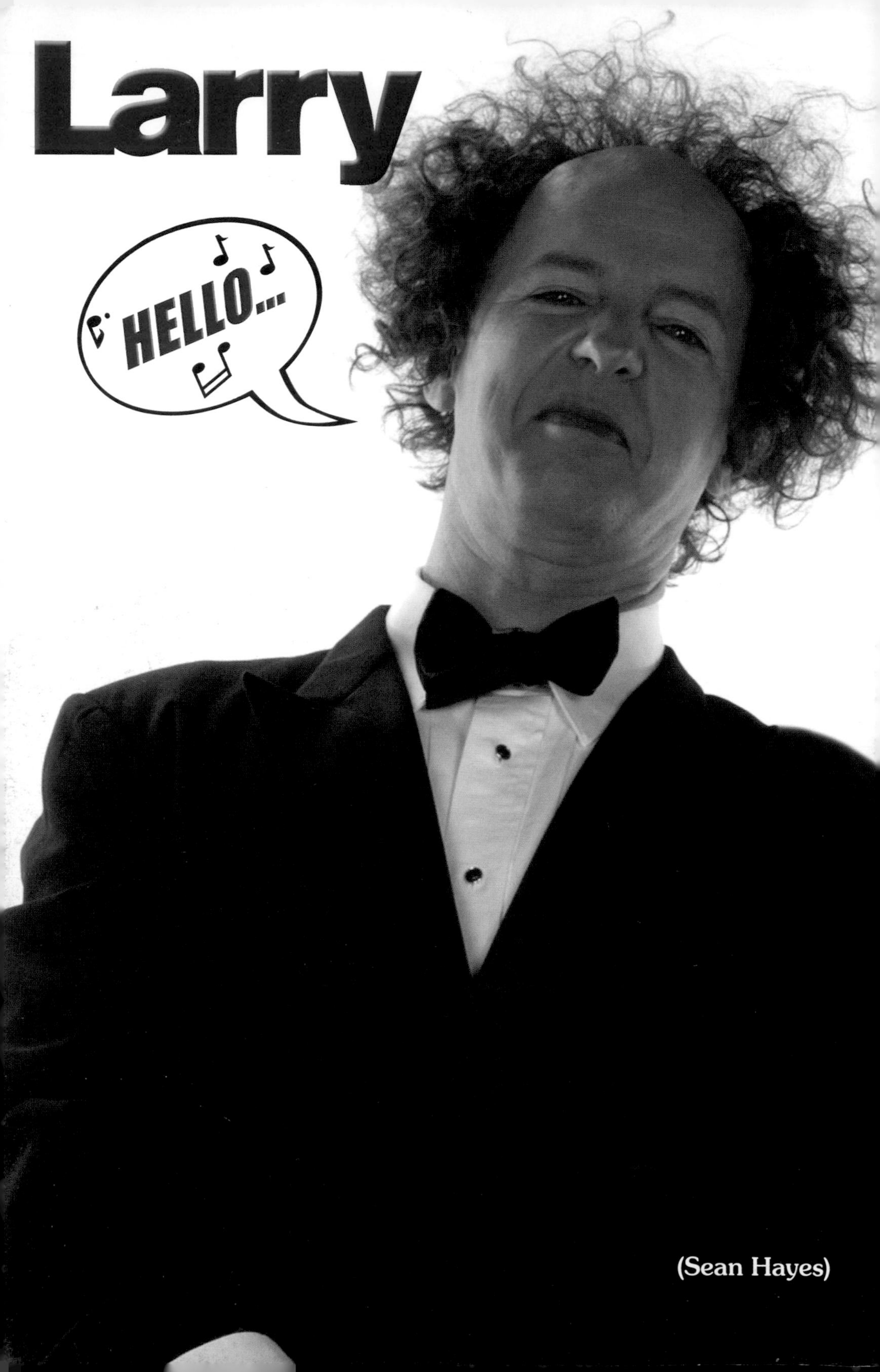
HELLO...

(Sean Hayes)

Curly

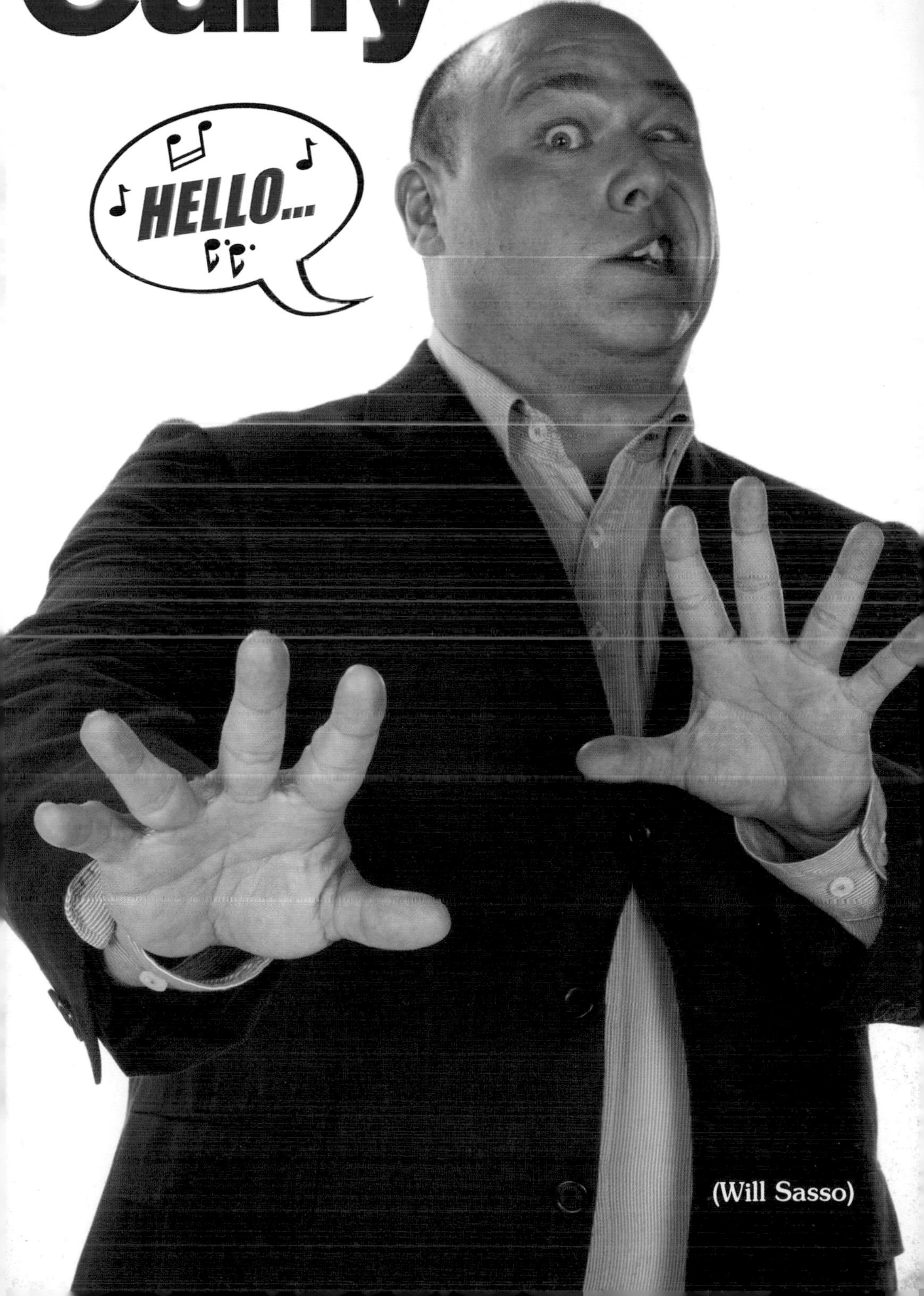
HELLO...

(Will Sasso)

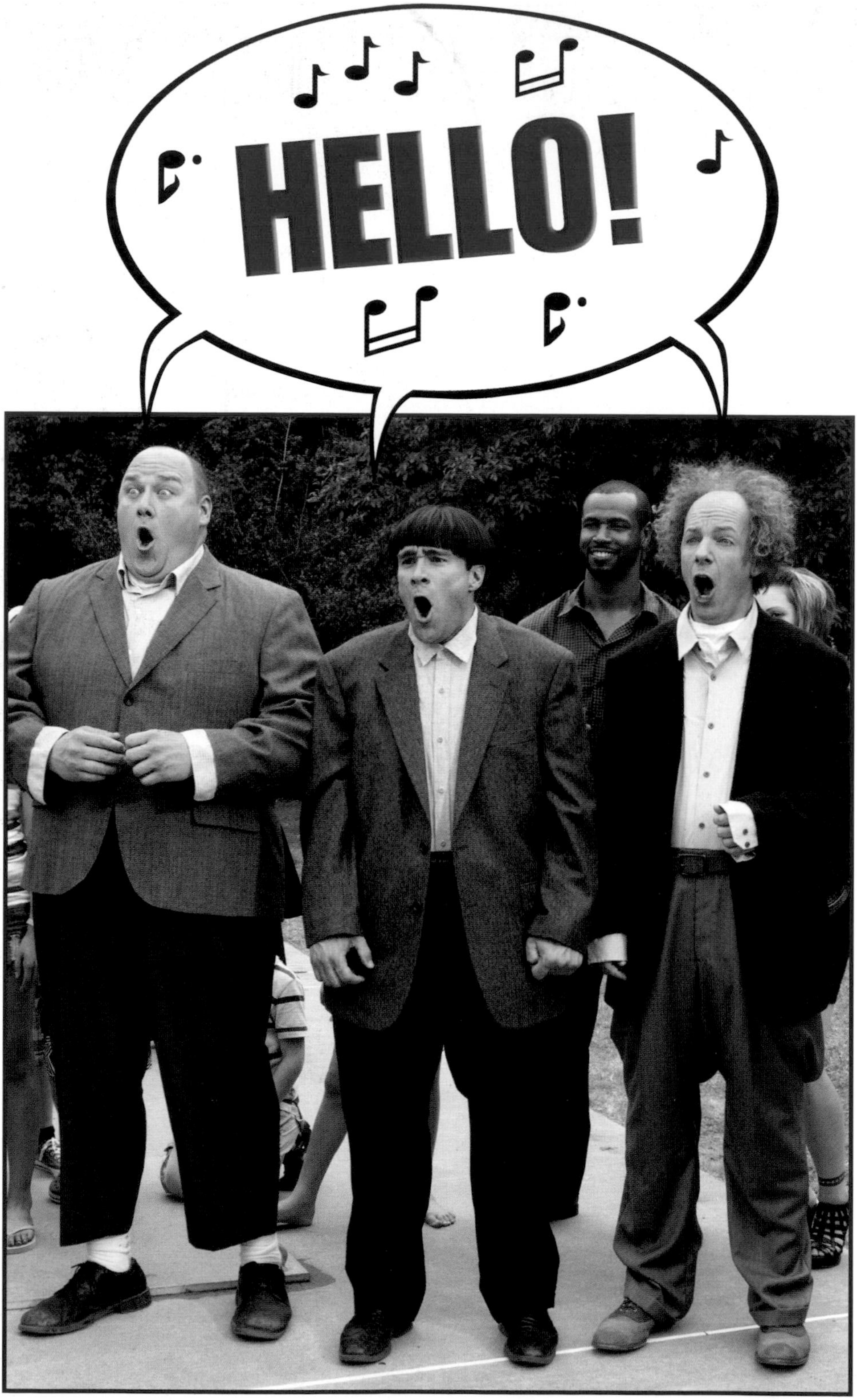
HELLO!

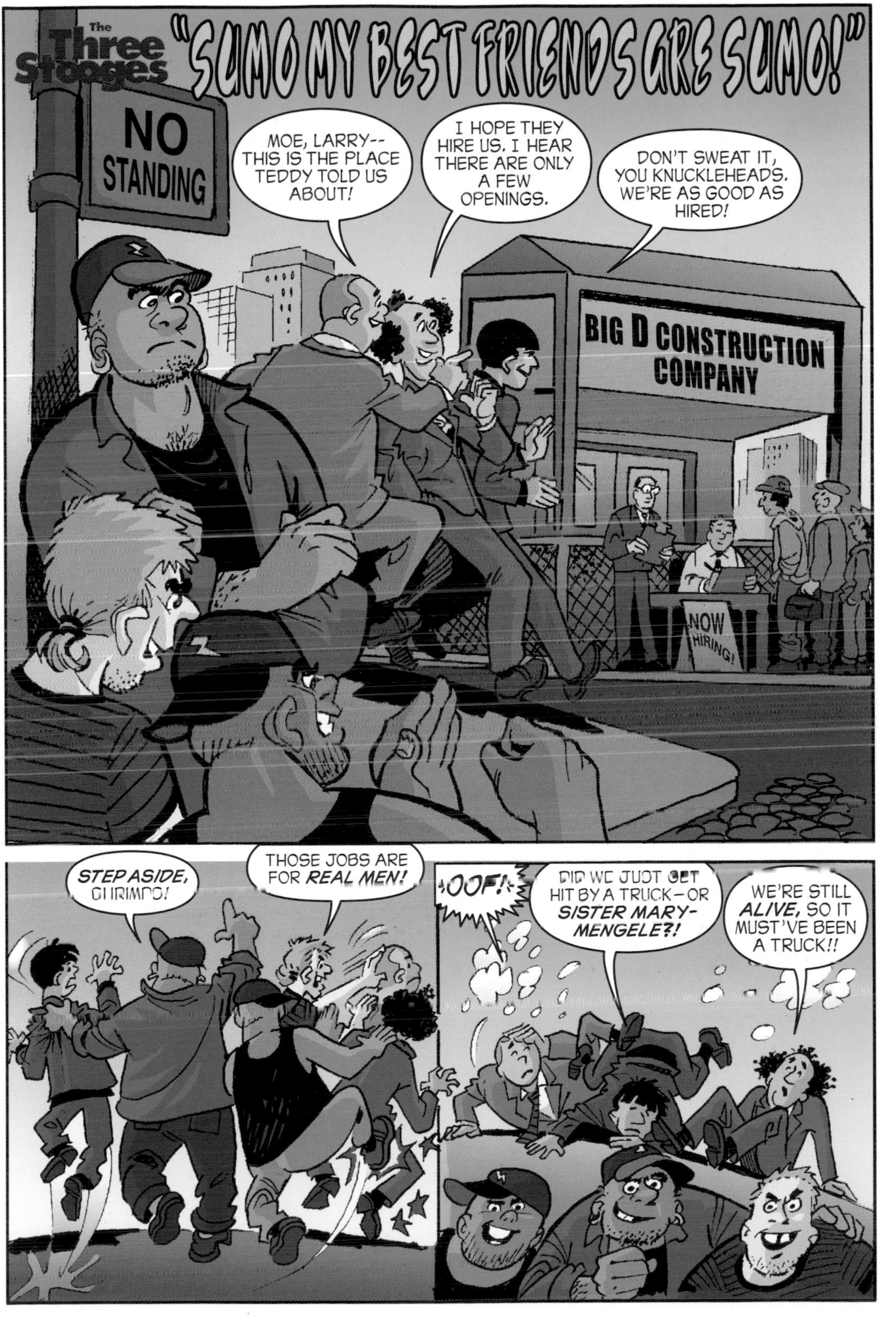
The Three Stooges
"SUMO MY BEST FRIENDS ARE SUMO!"
NO STANDING
MOE, LARRY-- THIS IS THE PLACE TEDDY TOLD US ABOUT!
I HOPE THEY HIRE US. I HEAR THERE ARE ONLY A FEW OPENINGS.
DON'T SWEAT IT, YOU KNUCKLEHEADS. WE'RE AS GOOD AS HIRED!
BIG D CONSTRUCTION COMPANY
NOW HIRING!
STEP ASIDE, SHRIMPS!
THOSE JOBS ARE FOR REAL MEN!
OOF!
DID WE JUST GET HIT BY A TRUCK—OR SISTER MARY-MENGELE?!
WE'RE STILL ALIVE, SO IT MUST'VE BEEN A TRUCK!!

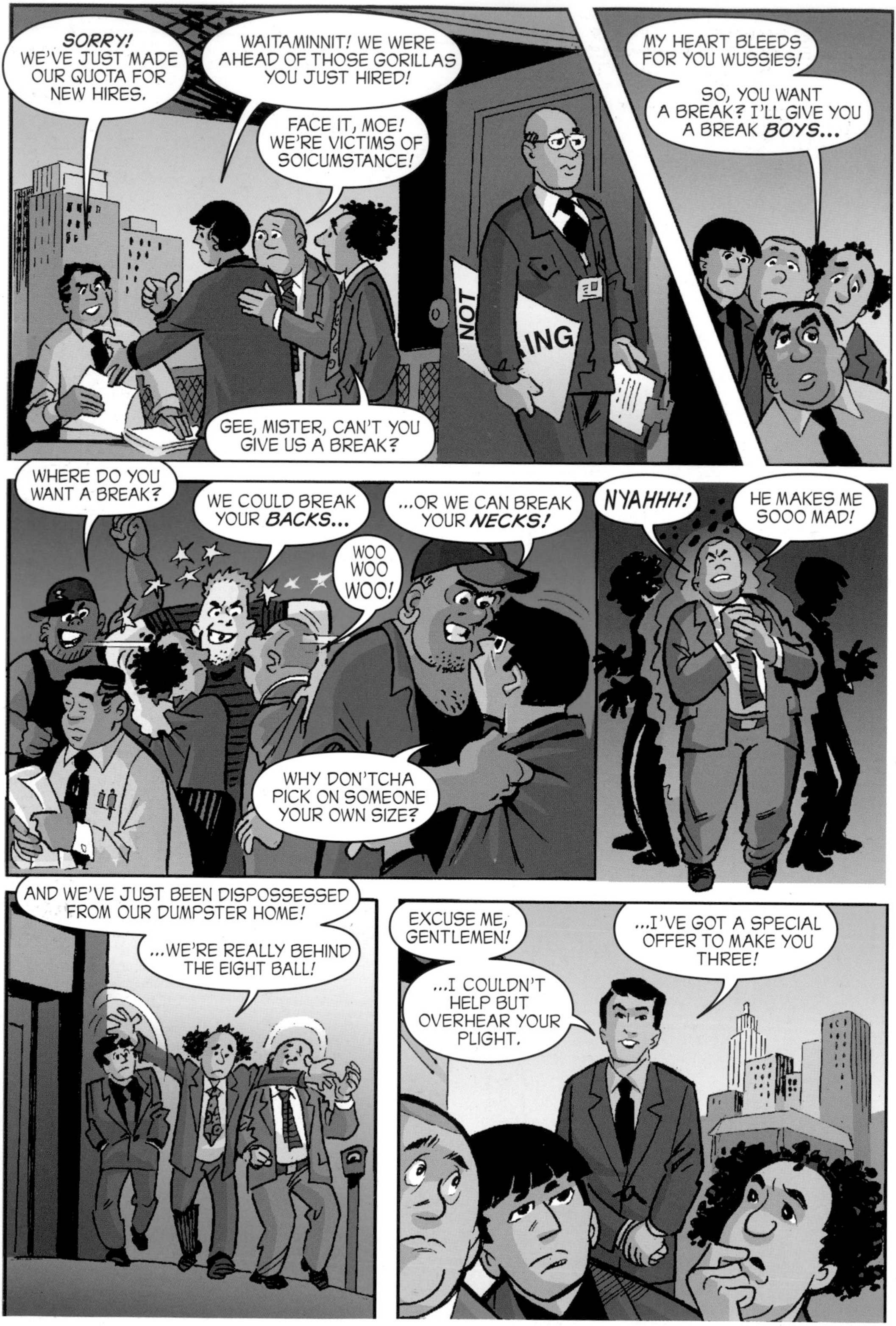
SORRY! WE'VE JUST MADE OUR QUOTA FOR NEW HIRES.
WAITAMINNIT! WE WERE AHEAD OF THOSE GORILLAS YOU JUST HIRED!
FACE IT, MOE! WE'RE VICTIMS OF SOICUMSTANCE!
GEE, MISTER, CAN'T YOU GIVE US A BREAK?
NOT
ING
MY HEART BLEEDS FOR YOU WUSSIES!
SO, YOU WANT A BREAK? I'LL GIVE YOU A BREAK BOYS...
WHERE DO YOU WANT A BREAK?
WE COULD BREAK YOUR BACKS...
...OR WE CAN BREAK YOUR NECKS!
WOO WOO WOO!
WHY DON'TCHA PICK ON SOMEONE YOUR OWN SIZE?
NYAHHH!
HE MAKES ME SOOO MAD!
AND WE'VE JUST BEEN DISPOSSESSED FROM OUR DUMPSTER HOME!
...WE'RE REALLY BEHIND THE EIGHT BALL!
EXCUSE ME, GENTLEMEN!
...I COULDN'T HELP BUT OVERHEAR YOUR PLIGHT.
...I'VE GOT A SPECIAL OFFER TO MAKE YOU THREE!

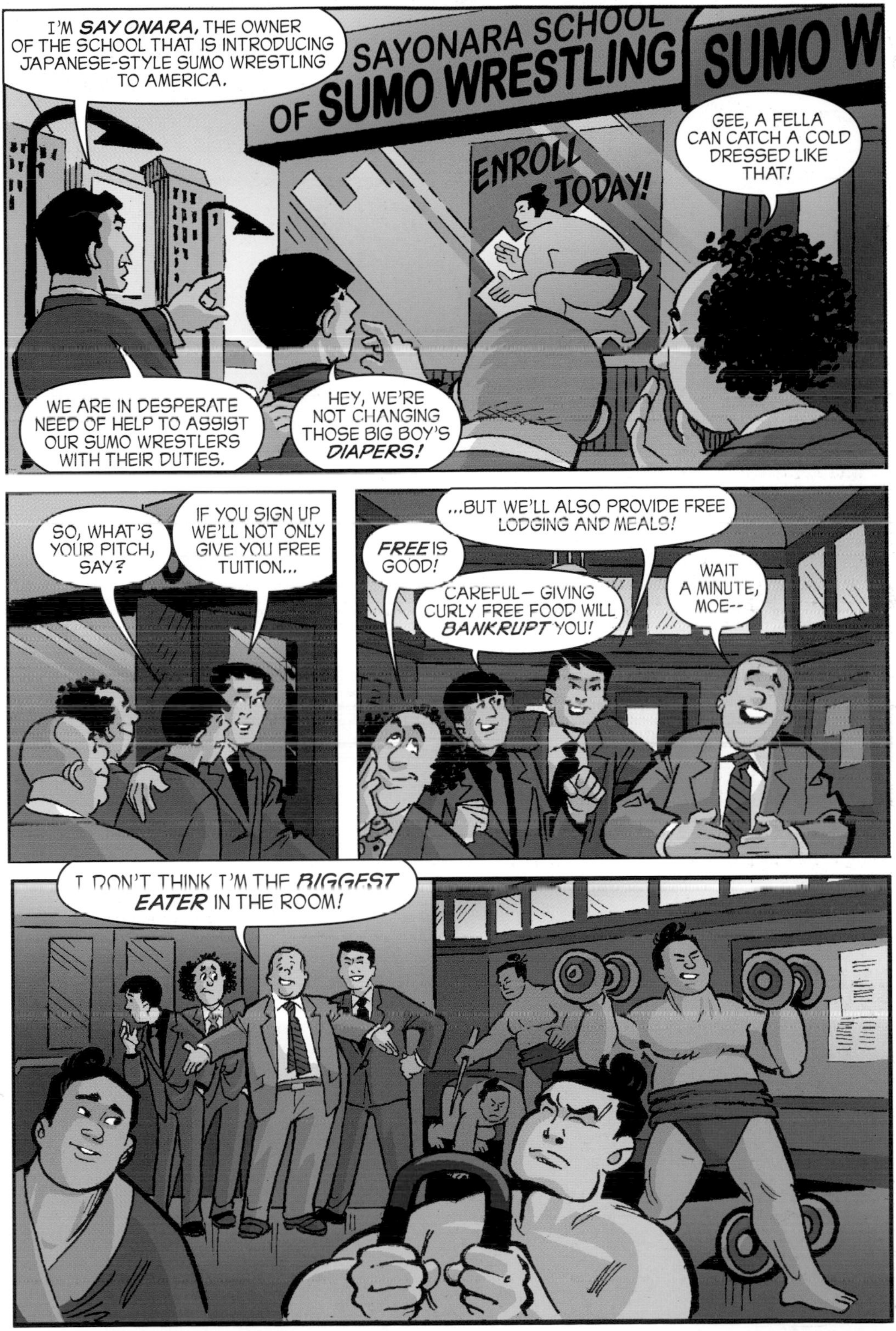
I'M SAYONARA, THE OWNER OF THE SCHOOL THAT IS INTRODUCING JAPANESE-STYLE SUMO WRESTLING TO AMERICA.
SAYONARA SCHOOL OF SUMO WRESTLING
SUMO W
ENROLL TODAY!
GEE, A FELLA CAN CATCH A COLD DRESSED LIKE THAT!
WE ARE IN DESPERATE NEED OF HELP TO ASSIST OUR SUMO WRESTLERS WITH THEIR DUTIES.
HEY, WE'RE NOT CHANGING THOSE BIG BOY'S DIAPERS!
SO, WHAT'S YOUR PITCH, SAY?
IF YOU SIGN UP WE'LL NOT ONLY GIVE YOU FREE TUITION...
...BUT WE'LL ALSO PROVIDE FREE LODGING AND MEALS!
FREE IS GOOD!
CAREFUL— GIVING CURLY FREE FOOD WILL BANKRUPT YOU!
WAIT A MINUTE, MOE--
I DON'T THINK I'M THE BIGGEST EATER IN THE ROOM!

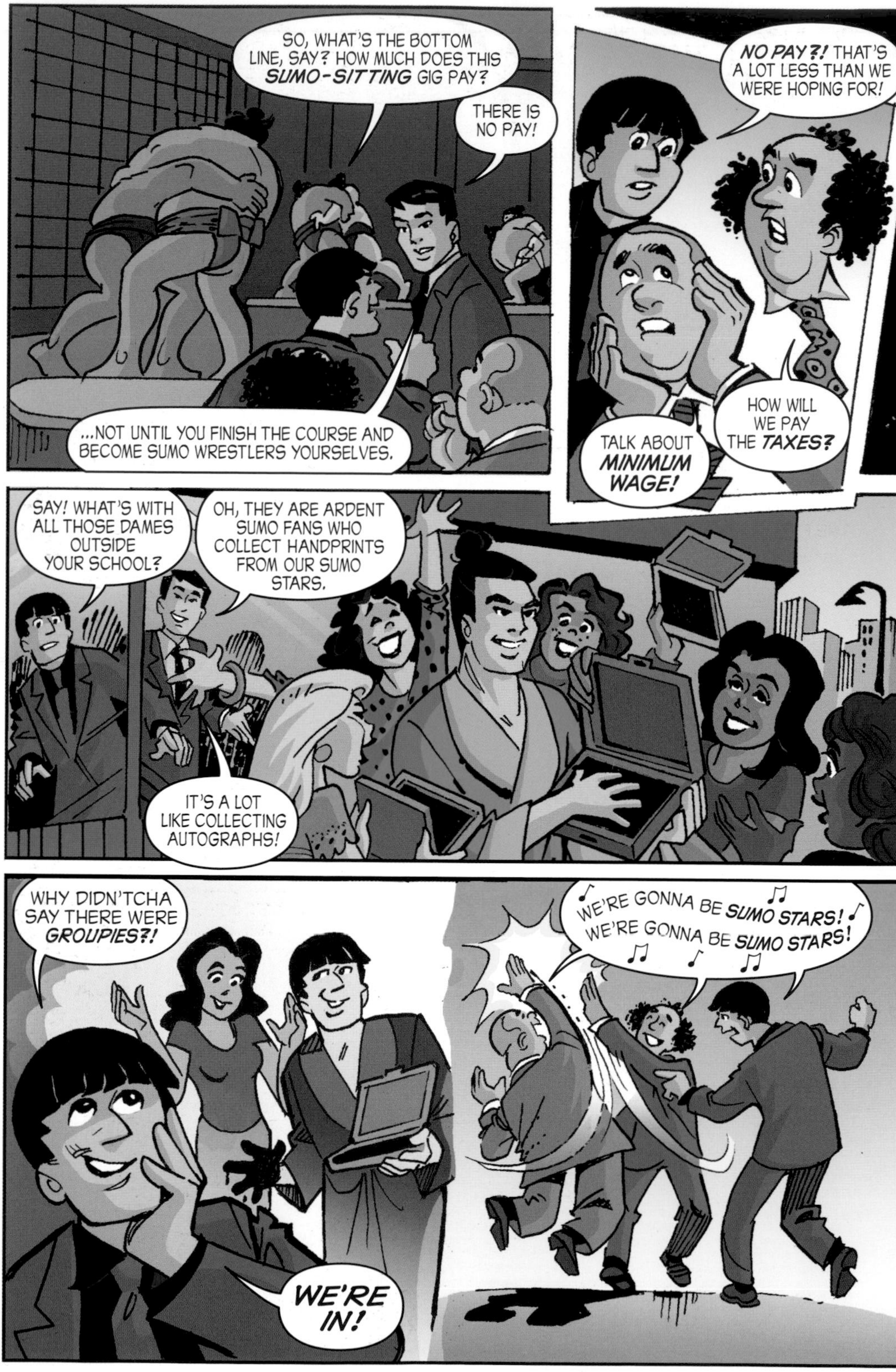
SO, WHAT'S THE BOTTOM LINE, SAY? HOW MUCH DOES THIS SUMO-SITTING GIG PAY?
THERE IS NO PAY!
...NOT UNTIL YOU FINISH THE COURSE AND BECOME SUMO WRESTLERS YOURSELVES.
NO PAY?! THAT'S A LOT LESS THAN WE WERE HOPING FOR!
HOW WILL WE PAY THE TAXES?
TALK ABOUT MINIMUM WAGE!
SAY! WHAT'S WITH ALL THOSE DAMES OUTSIDE YOUR SCHOOL?
OH, THEY ARE ARDENT SUMO FANS WHO COLLECT HANDPRINTS FROM OUR SUMO STARS.
IT'S A LOT LIKE COLLECTING AUTOGRAPHS!
WHY DIDN'TCHA SAY THERE WERE GROUPIES?!
WE'RE IN!
WE'RE GONNA BE SUMO STARS!
WE'RE GONNA BE SUMO STARS!

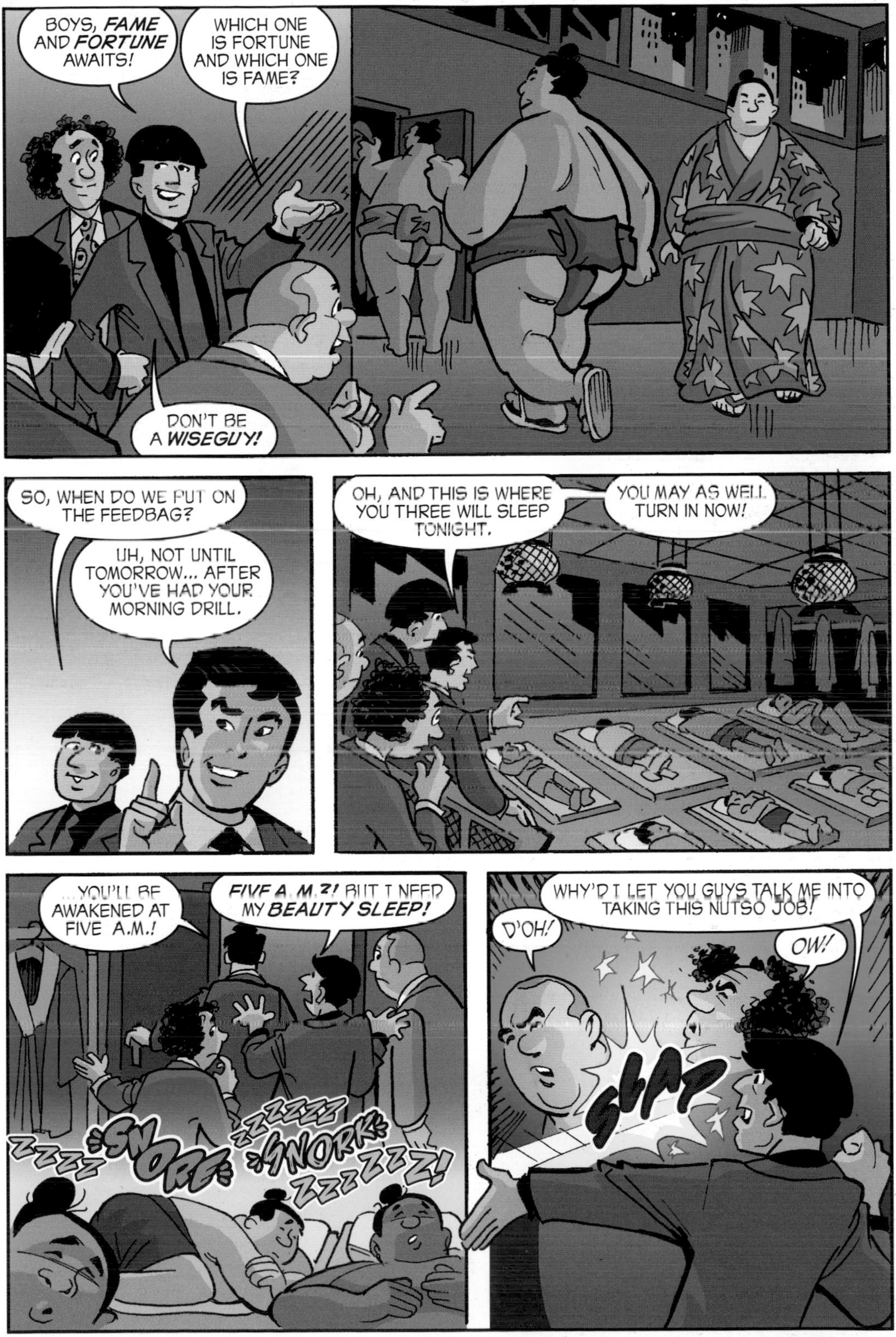

BOYS, FAME AND FORTUNE AWAITS!
WHICH ONE IS FORTUNE AND WHICH ONE IS FAME?
DON'T BE A WISEGUY!
SO, WHEN DO WE PUT ON THE FEEDBAG?
UH, NOT UNTIL TOMORROW... AFTER YOU'VE HAD YOUR MORNING DRILL.
OH, AND THIS IS WHERE YOU THREE WILL SLEEP TONIGHT.
YOU MAY AS WELL TURN IN NOW!
...YOU'LL BE AWAKENED AT FIVE A.M.!
FIVE A.M.?! BUT I NEED MY BEAUTY SLEEP!
ZZZZ SNORE ZZZZZZ SNORK ZZZZZZZ!
WHY'D I LET YOU GUYS TALK ME INTO TAKING THIS NUTSO JOB!
D'OH!
OW!
SLAP

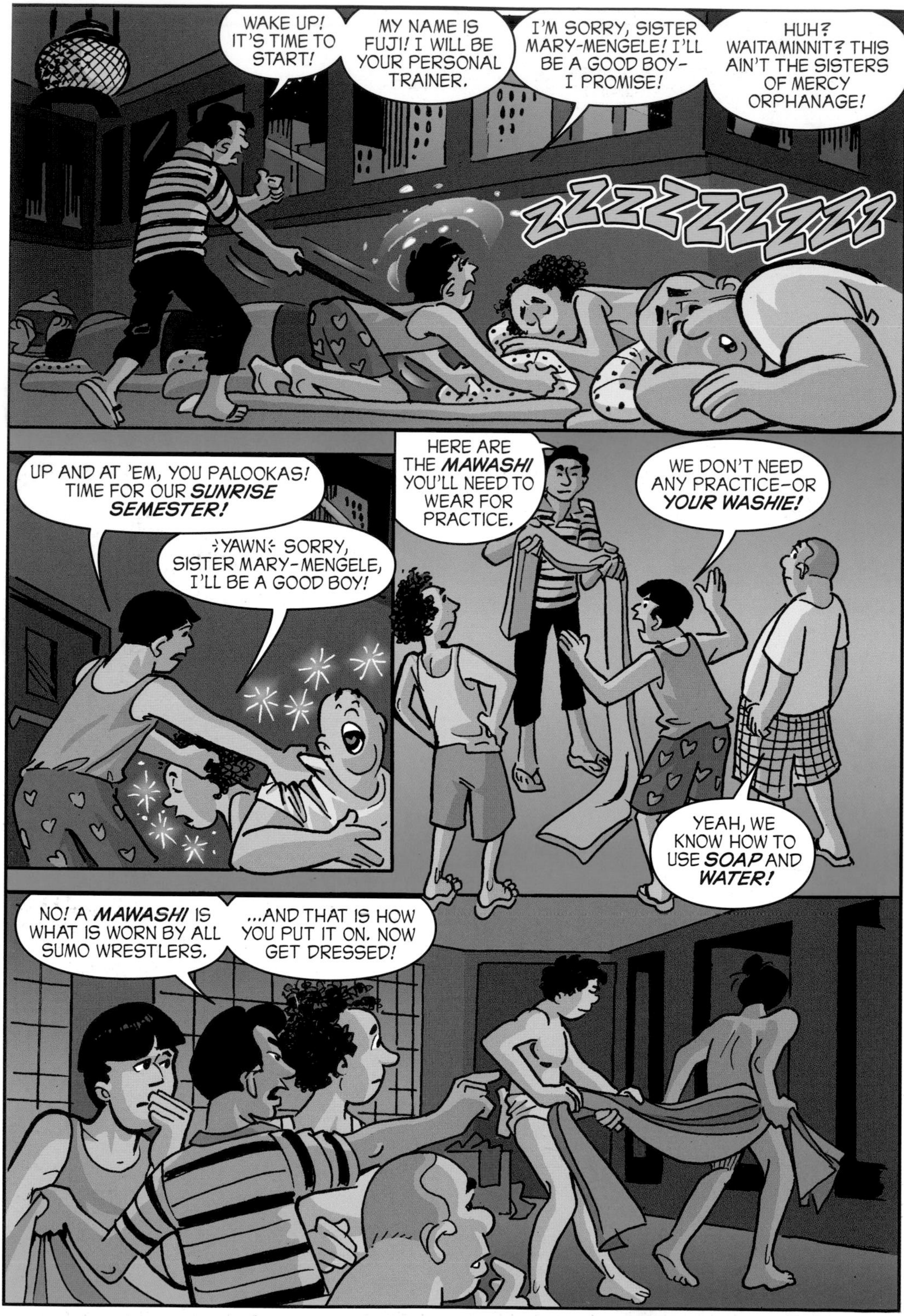
WAKE UP! IT'S TIME TO START!
MY NAME IS FUJI! I WILL BE YOUR PERSONAL TRAINER.
I'M SORRY, SISTER MARY-MENGELE! I'LL BE A GOOD BOY- I PROMISE!
HUH? WAITAMINNIT? THIS AIN'T THE SISTERS OF MERCY ORPHANAGE!
ZZZZZZZZZZZZ
UP AND AT 'EM, YOU PALOOKAS! TIME FOR OUR SUNRISE SEMESTER!
YAWN SORRY, SISTER MARY-MENGELE, I'LL BE A GOOD BOY!
HERE ARE THE MAWASHI YOU'LL NEED TO WEAR FOR PRACTICE.
WE DON'T NEED ANY PRACTICE—OR YOUR WASHIE!
YEAH, WE KNOW HOW TO USE SOAP AND WATER!
NO! A MAWASHI IS WHAT IS WORN BY ALL SUMO WRESTLERS.
...AND THAT IS HOW YOU PUT IT ON. NOW GET DRESSED!

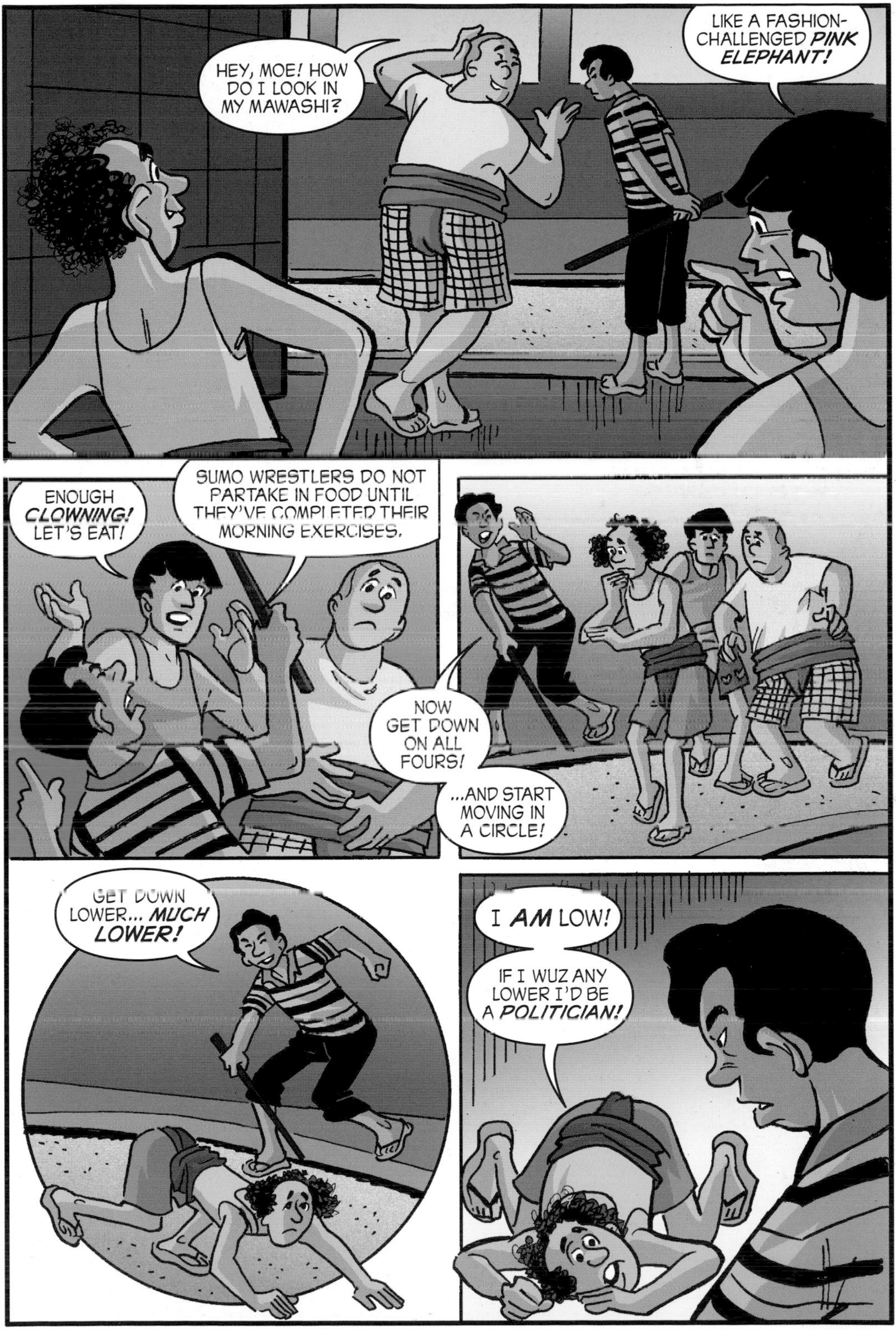
HEY, MOE! HOW DO I LOOK IN MY MAWASHI?
LIKE A FASHION-CHALLENGED PINK ELEPHANT!
ENOUGH CLOWNING! LET'S EAT!
SUMO WRESTLERS DO NOT PARTAKE IN FOOD UNTIL THEY'VE COMPLETED THEIR MORNING EXERCISES.
NOW GET DOWN ON ALL FOURS!
...AND START MOVING IN A CIRCLE!
GET DOWN LOWER... MUCH LOWER!
I AM LOW!
IF I WUZ ANY LOWER I'D BE A POLITICIAN!

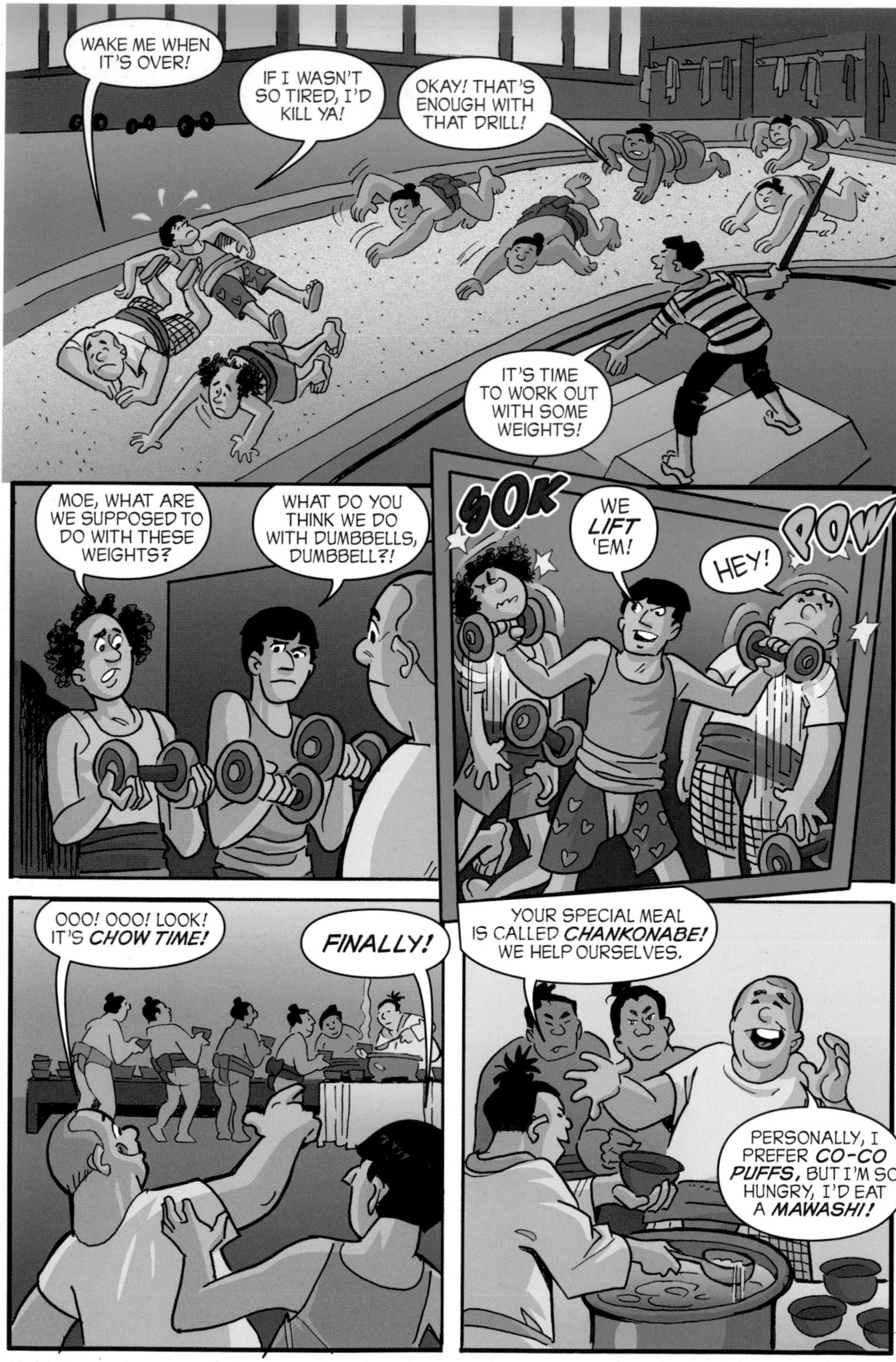
WAKE ME WHEN IT'S OVER!
IF I WASN'T SO TIRED, I'D KILL YA!
OKAY! THAT'S ENOUGH WITH THAT DRILL!
IT'S TIME TO WORK OUT WITH SOME WEIGHTS!
MOE, WHAT ARE WE SUPPOSED TO DO WITH THESE WEIGHTS?
WHAT DO YOU THINK WE DO WITH DUMBBELLS, DUMBBELL?!
SOK
WE LIFT 'EM!
HEY!
POW
OOO! OOO! LOOK! IT'S CHOW TIME!
FINALLY!
YOUR SPECIAL MEAL IS CALLED CHANKONABE! WE HELP OURSELVES.
PERSONALLY, I PREFER CO-CO PUFFS, BUT I'M SO HUNGRY, I'D EAT A MAWASHI!

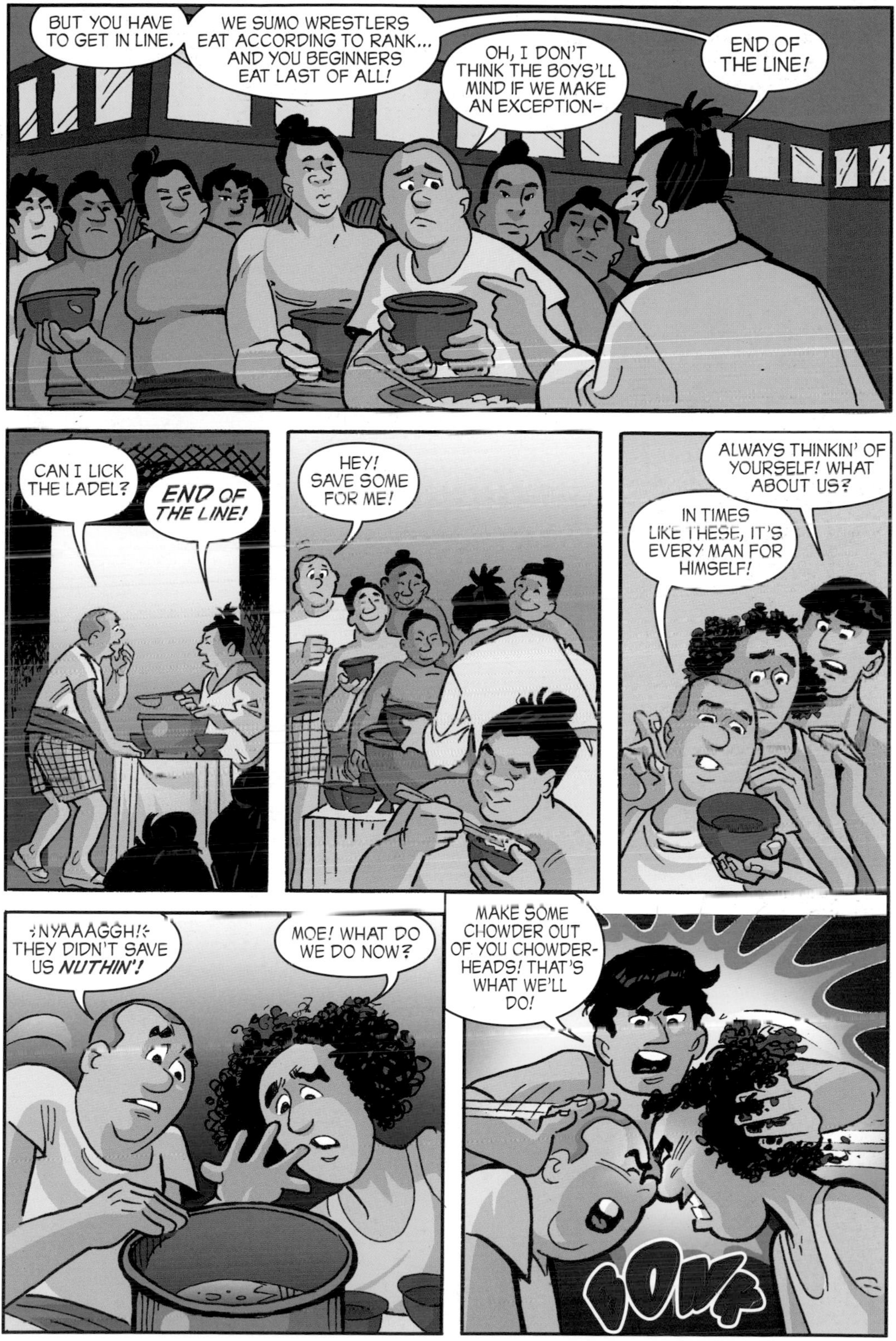
BUT YOU HAVE TO GET IN LINE.
WE SUMO WRESTLERS EAT ACCORDING TO RANK... AND YOU BEGINNERS EAT LAST OF ALL!
OH, I DON'T THINK THE BOYS'LL MIND IF WE MAKE AN EXCEPTION-
END OF THE LINE!
CAN I LICK THE LADEL?
END OF THE LINE!
HEY! SAVE SOME FOR ME!
ALWAYS THINKIN' OF YOURSELF! WHAT ABOUT US?
IN TIMES LIKE THESE, IT'S EVERY MAN FOR HIMSELF!
NYAAAGGH! THEY DIDN'T SAVE US NUTHIN'!
MOE! WHAT DO WE DO NOW?
MAKE SOME CHOWDER OUT OF YOU CHOWDER-HEADS! THAT'S WHAT WE'LL DO!
BONK

IT'S TIME TO GET BACK TO OUR WORKOUT. I NEED A VOLUNTEER...

PICK ME! I VOLUNTEER!

THE STRATEGY OF SUMO IS VERY SIMPLE!

IT'S TO PUSH, SHOVE, OR THROW YOUR OPPONENT OUT OF THE RING.

...AND SOMETIMES ONE CAN EVEN KNOCK AN OPPONENT OUT OF THE RING WITHOUT USING HIS HANDS.

NO HANDS? HOW IS THAT POSSIBLE?

BY EATING LOTS AND LOTS OF CABBAGE BEFORE THE MATCH.

THERE WAS CABBBAGE?

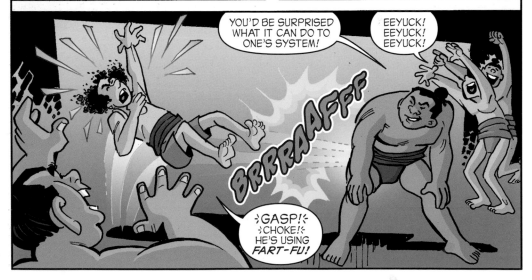

YOU'D BE SURPRISED WHAT IT CAN DO TO ONE'S SYSTEM!

EEYUCK! EEYUCK! EEYUCK!

BRRRAAFPF

GASP! *CHOKE!* HE'S USING FART-FU!

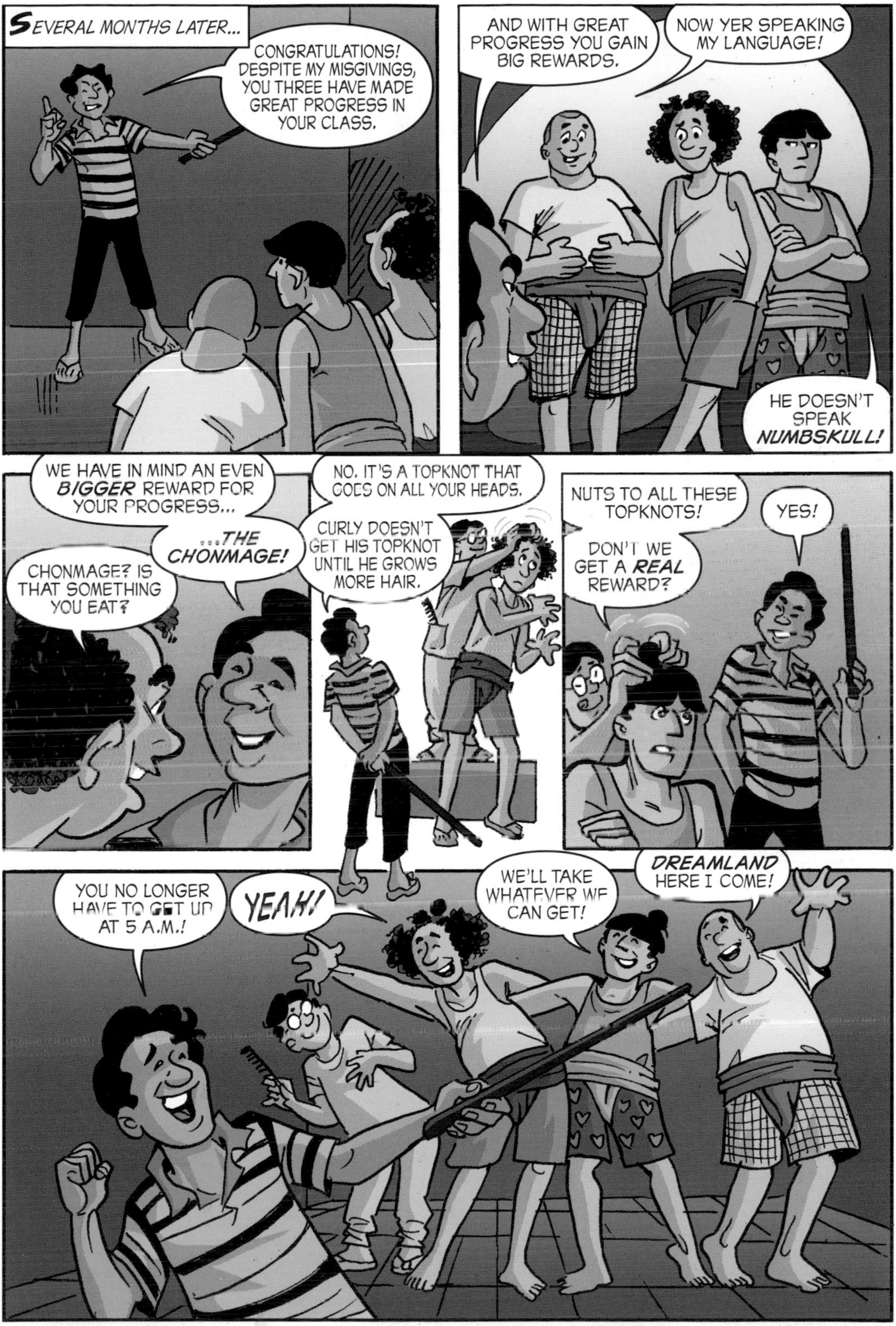
SEVERAL MONTHS LATER...
CONGRATULATIONS! DESPITE MY MISGIVINGS, YOU THREE HAVE MADE GREAT PROGRESS IN YOUR CLASS.
AND WITH GREAT PROGRESS YOU GAIN BIG REWARDS.
NOW YER SPEAKING MY LANGUAGE!
HE DOESN'T SPEAK NUMBSKULL!
WE HAVE IN MIND AN EVEN BIGGER REWARD FOR YOUR PROGRESS...
...THE CHONMAGE!
CHONMAGE? IS THAT SOMETHING YOU EAT?
NO. IT'S A TOPKNOT THAT GOES ON ALL YOUR HEADS.
CURLY DOESN'T GET HIS TOPKNOT UNTIL HE GROWS MORE HAIR.
NUTS TO ALL THESE TOPKNOTS!
DON'T WE GET A REAL REWARD?
YES!
YOU NO LONGER HAVE TO GET UP AT 5 A.M.!
YEAH!
WE'LL TAKE WHATEVER WE CAN GET!
DREAMLAND HERE I COME!

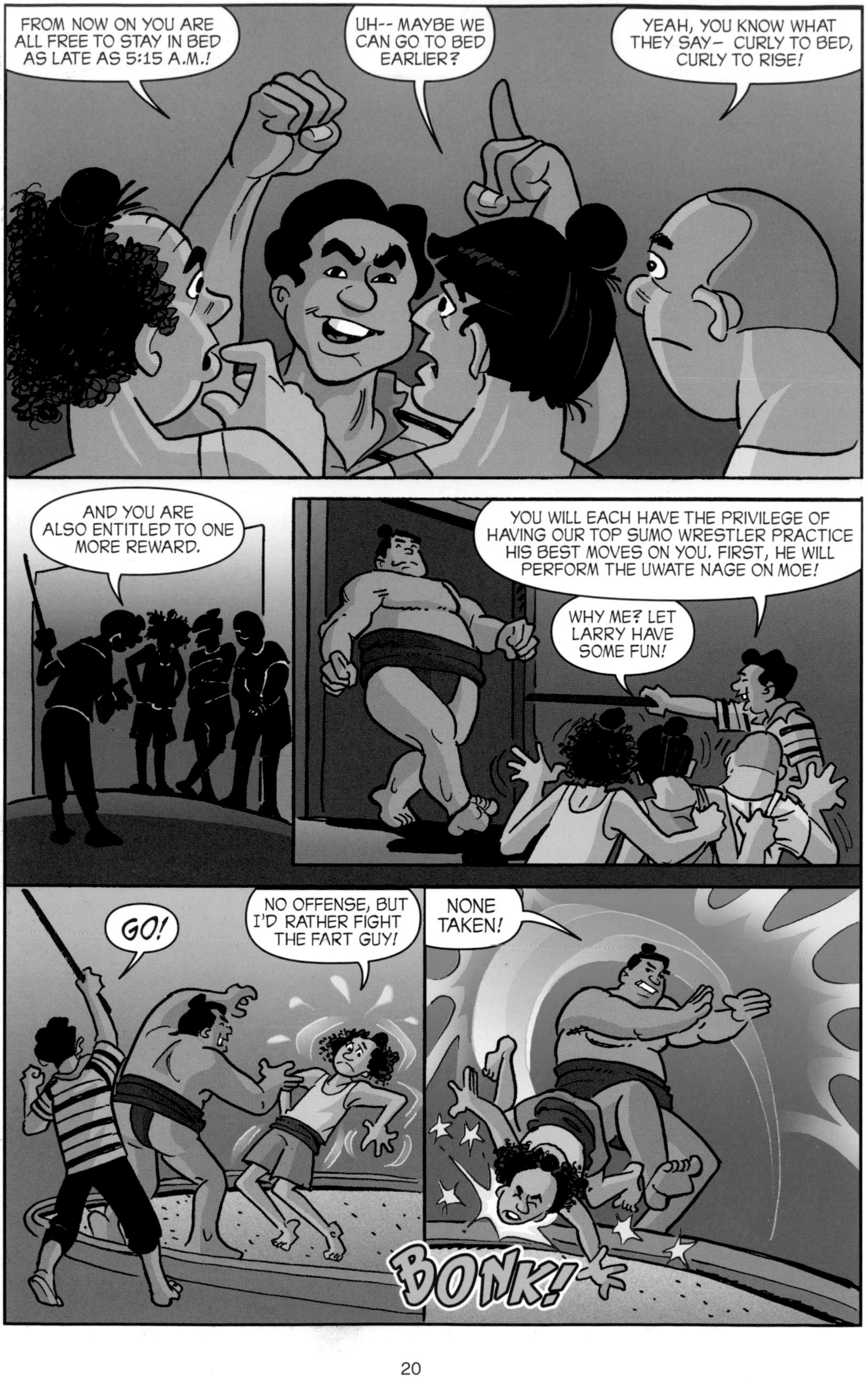
FROM NOW ON YOU ARE ALL FREE TO STAY IN BED AS LATE AS 5:15 A.M.!
UH-- MAYBE WE CAN GO TO BED EARLIER?
YEAH, YOU KNOW WHAT THEY SAY– CURLY TO BED, CURLY TO RISE!
AND YOU ARE ALSO ENTITLED TO ONE MORE REWARD.
YOU WILL EACH HAVE THE PRIVILEGE OF HAVING OUR TOP SUMO WRESTLER PRACTICE HIS BEST MOVES ON YOU. FIRST, HE WILL PERFORM THE UWATE NAGE ON MOE!
WHY ME? LET LARRY HAVE SOME FUN!
GO!
NO OFFENSE, BUT I'D RATHER FIGHT THE FART GUY!
NONE TAKEN!
BONK!

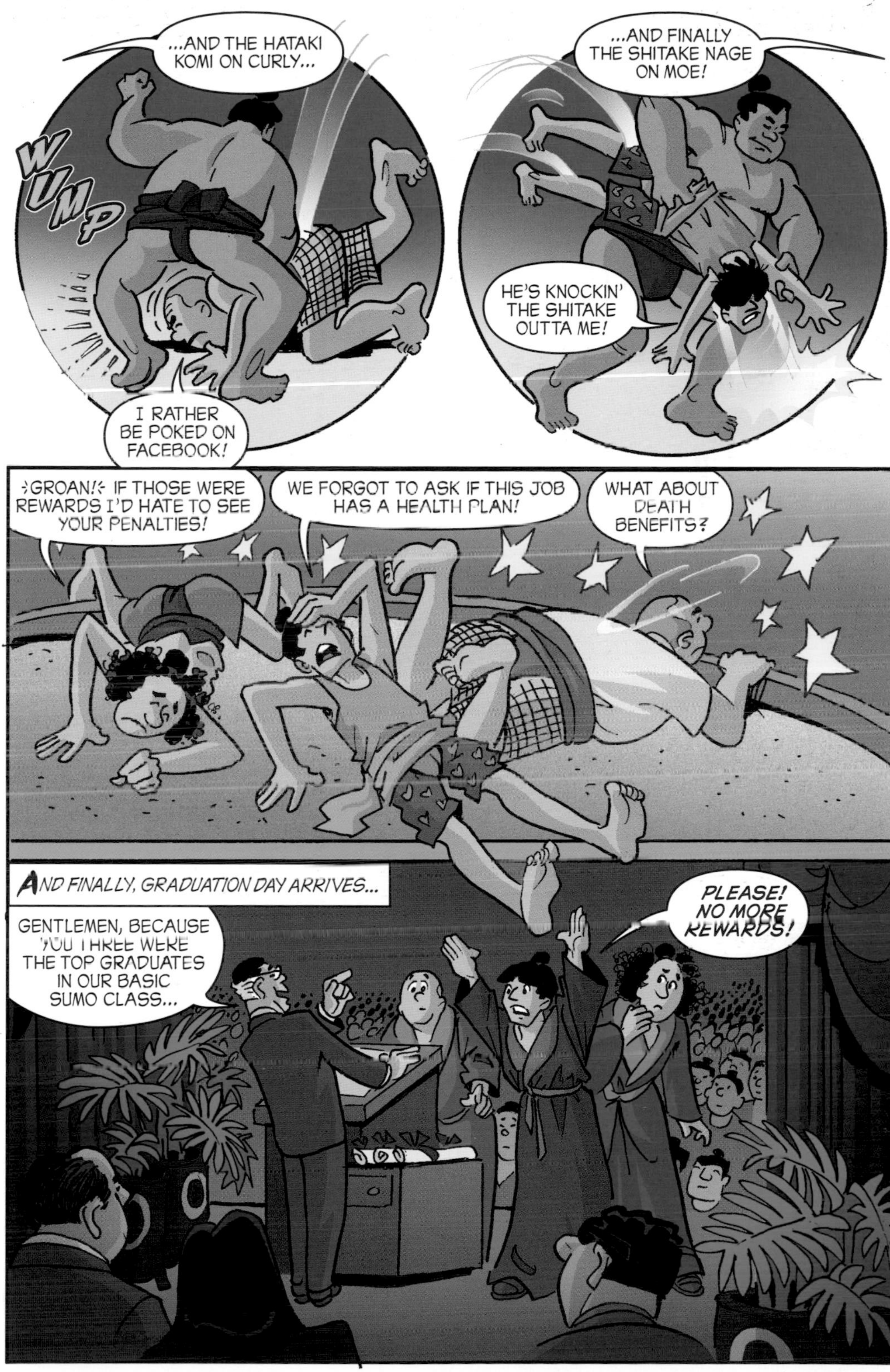

...AND THE HATAKI KOMI ON CURLY...
WUMP
I RATHER BE POKED ON FACEBOOK!
...AND FINALLY THE SHITAKE NAGE ON MOE!
HE'S KNOCKIN' THE SHITAKE OUTTA ME!
GROAN! IF THOSE WERE REWARDS I'D HATE TO SEE YOUR PENALTIES!
WE FORGOT TO ASK IF THIS JOB HAS A HEALTH PLAN!
WHAT ABOUT DEATH BENEFITS?
AND FINALLY, GRADUATION DAY ARRIVES...
GENTLEMEN, BECAUSE YOU THREE WERE THE TOP GRADUATES IN OUR BASIC SUMO CLASS...
PLEASE! NO MORE REWARDS!

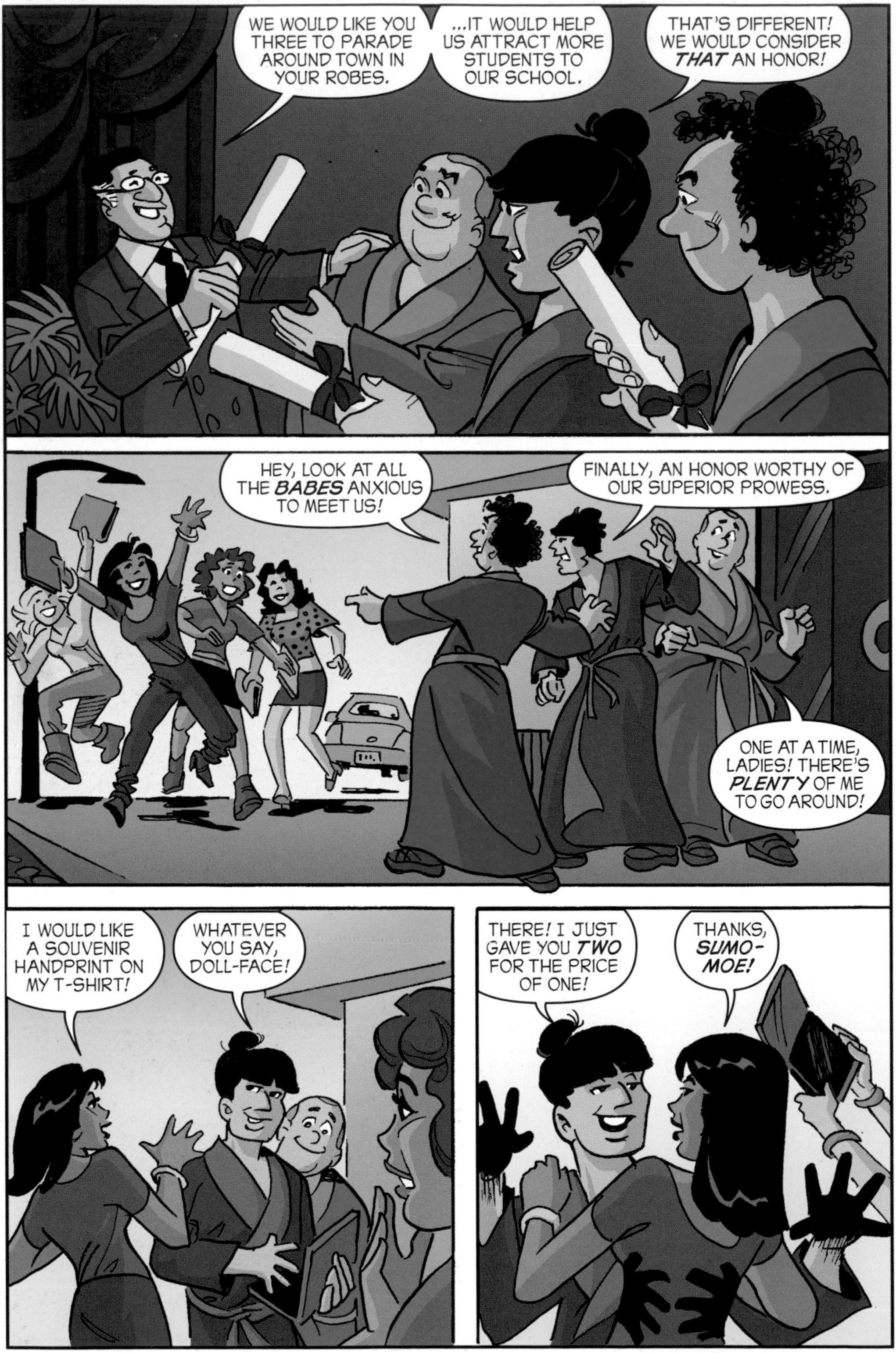
WE WOULD LIKE YOU THREE TO PARADE AROUND TOWN IN YOUR ROBES.
...IT WOULD HELP US ATTRACT MORE STUDENTS TO OUR SCHOOL.
THAT'S DIFFERENT! WE WOULD CONSIDER *THAT* AN HONOR!
HEY, LOOK AT ALL THE *BABES* ANXIOUS TO MEET US!
FINALLY, AN HONOR WORTHY OF OUR SUPERIOR PROWESS.
ONE AT A TIME, LADIES! THERE'S *PLENTY* OF ME TO GO AROUND!
I WOULD LIKE A SOUVENIR HANDPRINT ON MY T-SHIRT!
WHATEVER YOU SAY, DOLL-FACE!
THERE! I JUST GAVE YOU *TWO* FOR THE PRICE OF ONE!
THANKS, *SUMO-MOE!*

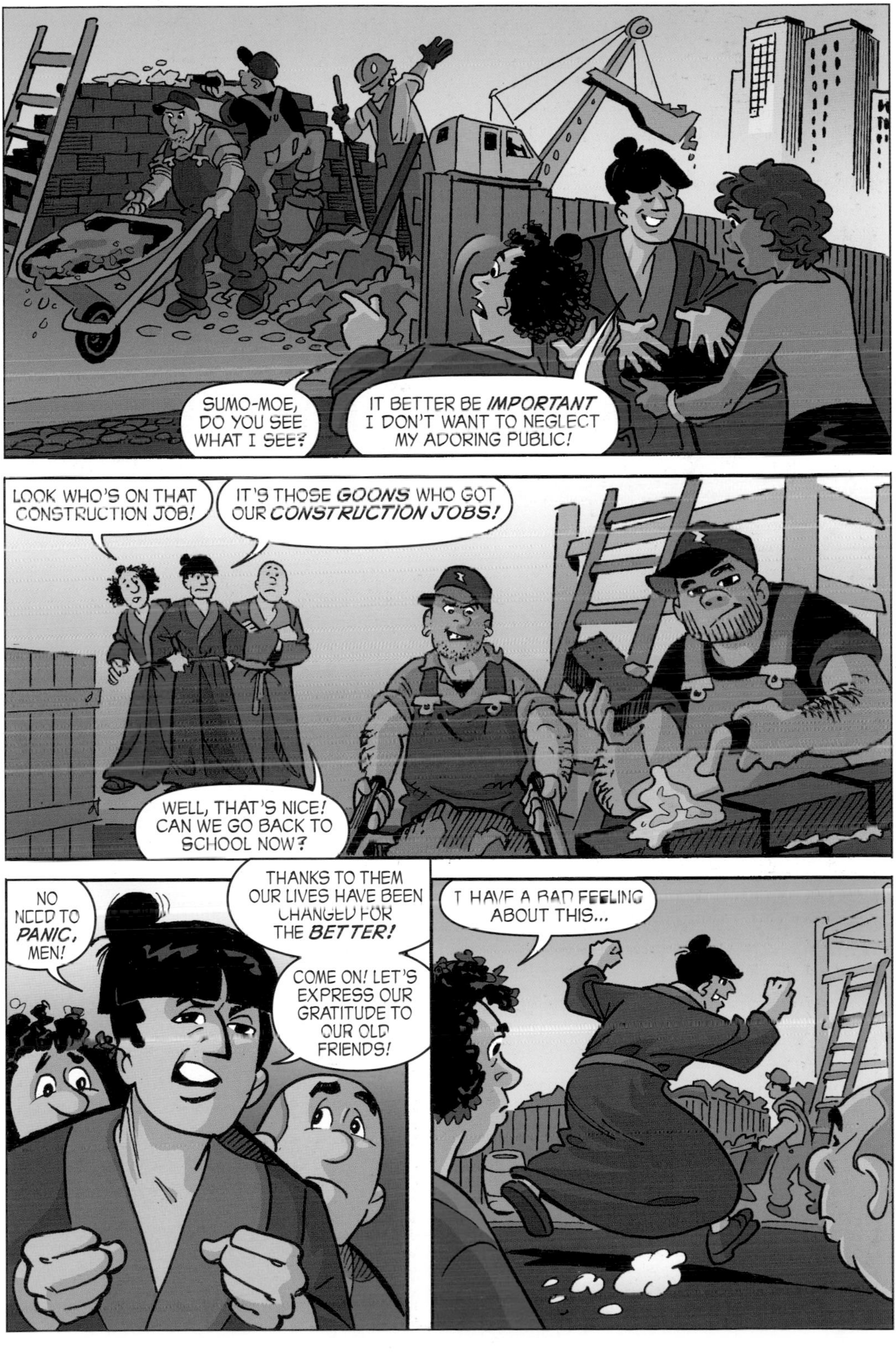
SUMO-MOE, DO YOU SEE WHAT I SEE?
IT BETTER BE IMPORTANT I DON'T WANT TO NEGLECT MY ADORING PUBLIC!
LOOK WHO'S ON THAT CONSTRUCTION JOB!
IT'S THOSE GOONS WHO GOT OUR CONSTRUCTION JOBS!
WELL, THAT'S NICE! CAN WE GO BACK TO SCHOOL NOW?
NO NEED TO PANIC, MEN!
THANKS TO THEM OUR LIVES HAVE BEEN CHANGED FOR THE BETTER!
COME ON! LET'S EXPRESS OUR GRATITUDE TO OUR OLD FRIENDS!
I HAVE A BAD FEELING ABOUT THIS...

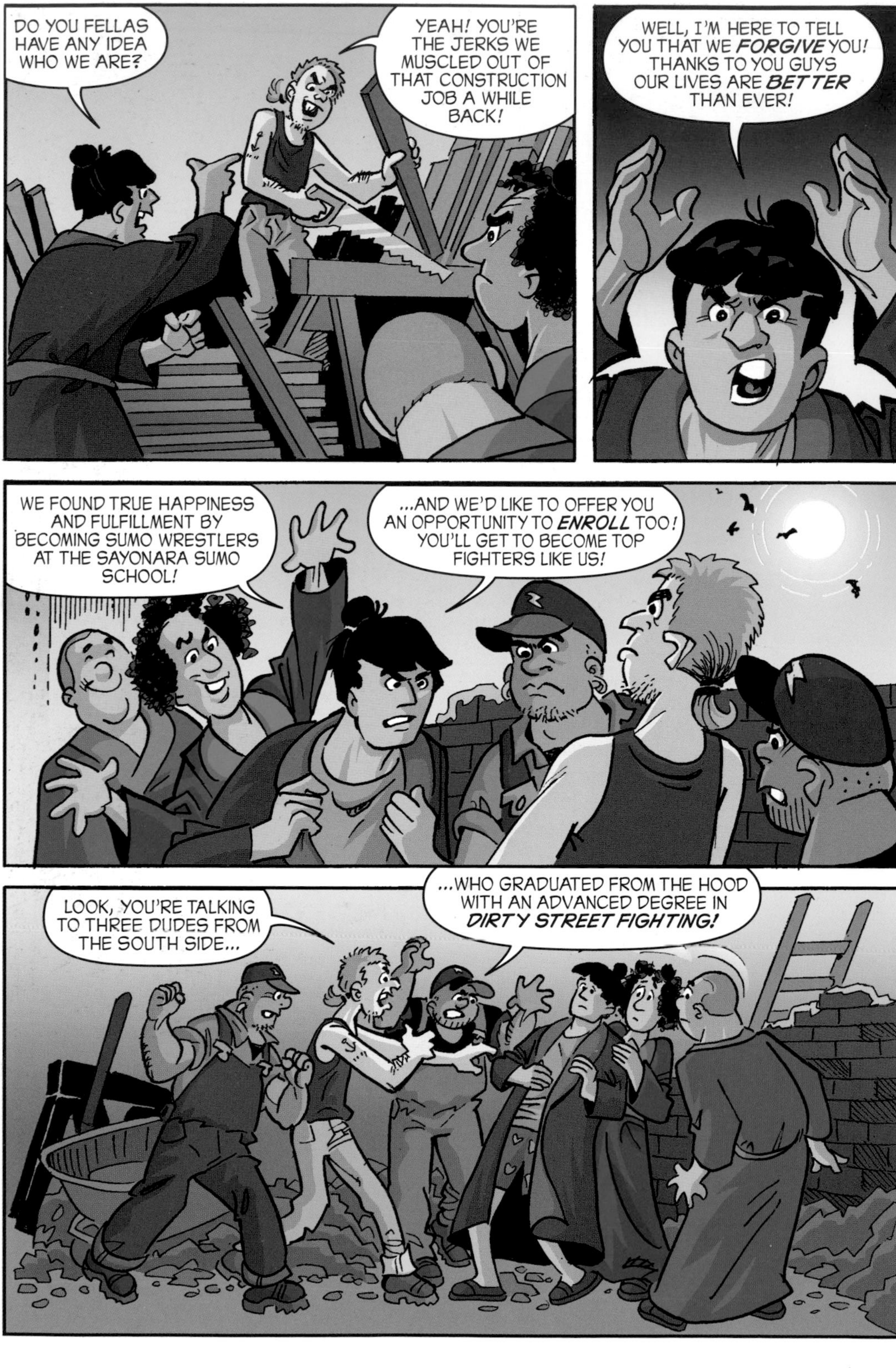
DO YOU FELLAS HAVE ANY IDEA WHO WE ARE?
YEAH! YOU'RE THE JERKS WE MUSCLED OUT OF THAT CONSTRUCTION JOB A WHILE BACK!
WELL, I'M HERE TO TELL YOU THAT WE FORGIVE YOU! THANKS TO YOU GUYS OUR LIVES ARE BETTER THAN EVER!
WE FOUND TRUE HAPPINESS AND FULFILLMENT BY BECOMING SUMO WRESTLERS AT THE SAYONARA SUMO SCHOOL!
...AND WE'D LIKE TO OFFER YOU AN OPPORTUNITY TO ENROLL TOO! YOU'LL GET TO BECOME TOP FIGHTERS LIKE US!
LOOK, YOU'RE TALKING TO THREE DUDES FROM THE SOUTH SIDE...
...WHO GRADUATED FROM THE HOOD WITH AN ADVANCED DEGREE IN DIRTY STREET FIGHTING!

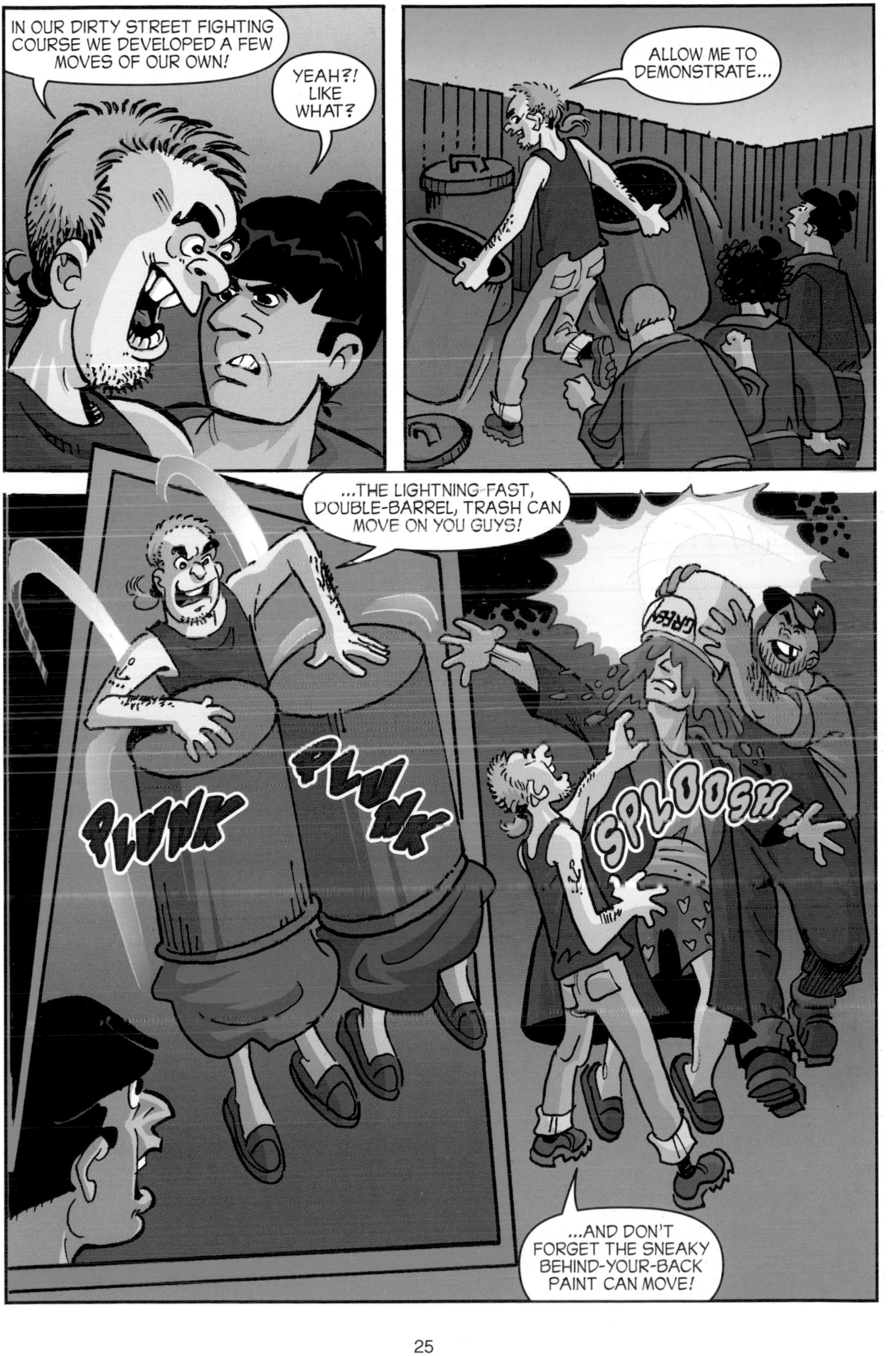
IN OUR DIRTY STREET FIGHTING COURSE WE DEVELOPED A FEW MOVES OF OUR OWN!
YEAH?! LIKE WHAT?
ALLOW ME TO DEMONSTRATE...
...THE LIGHTNING-FAST, DOUBLE-BARREL, TRASH CAN MOVE ON YOU GUYS!
PLUNK
PLUNK
SPLOOSH
...AND DON'T FORGET THE SNEAKY BEHIND-YOUR-BACK PAINT CAN MOVE!

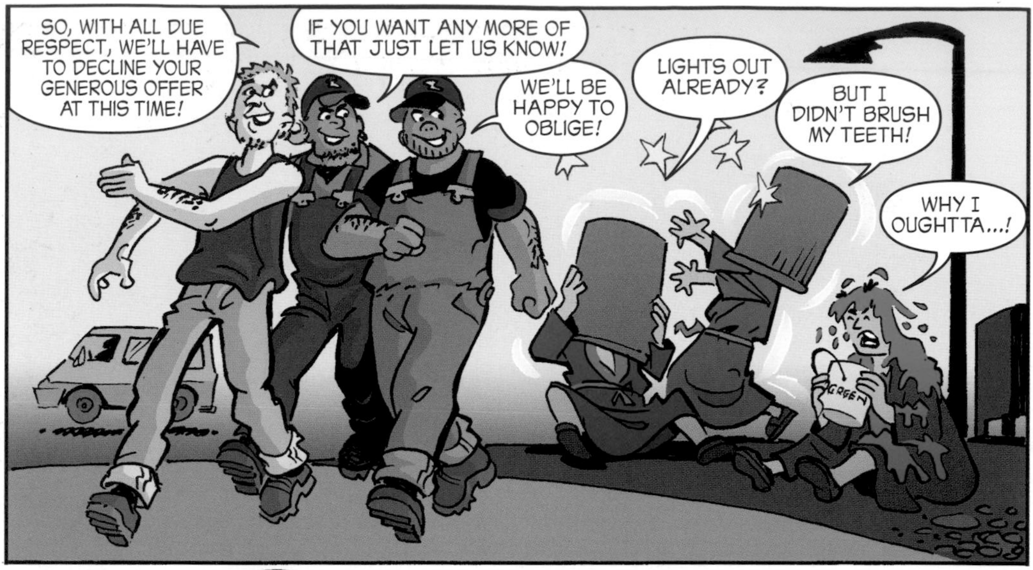
SO, WITH ALL DUE RESPECT, WE'LL HAVE TO DECLINE YOUR GENEROUS OFFER AT THIS TIME!
IF YOU WANT ANY MORE OF THAT JUST LET US KNOW!
WE'LL BE HAPPY TO OBLIGE!
LIGHTS OUT ALREADY?
BUT I DIDN'T BRUSH MY TEETH!
WHY I OUGHTTA...!
GREEN

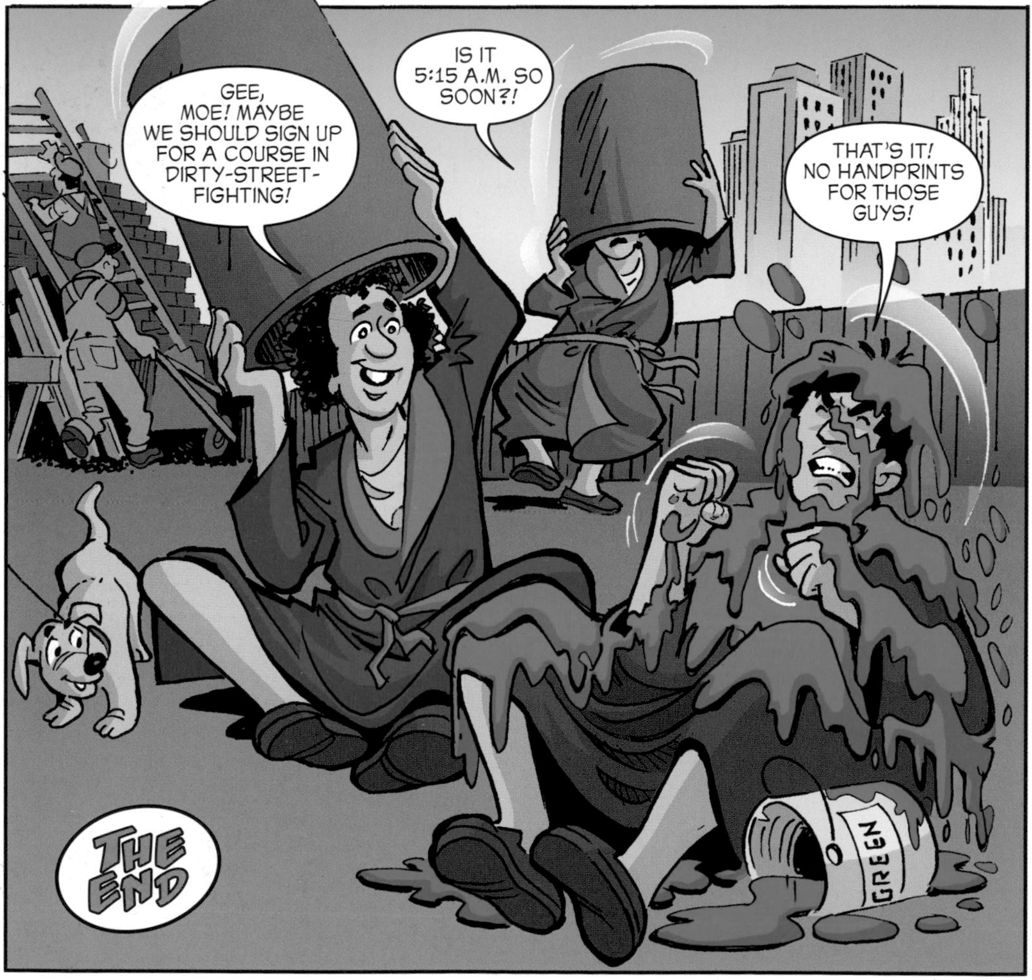
GEE, MOE! MAYBE WE SHOULD SIGN UP FOR A COURSE IN DIRTY-STREET-FIGHTING!
IS IT 5:15 A.M. SO SOON?!
THAT'S IT! NO HANDPRINTS FOR THOSE GUYS!
THE END
GREEN

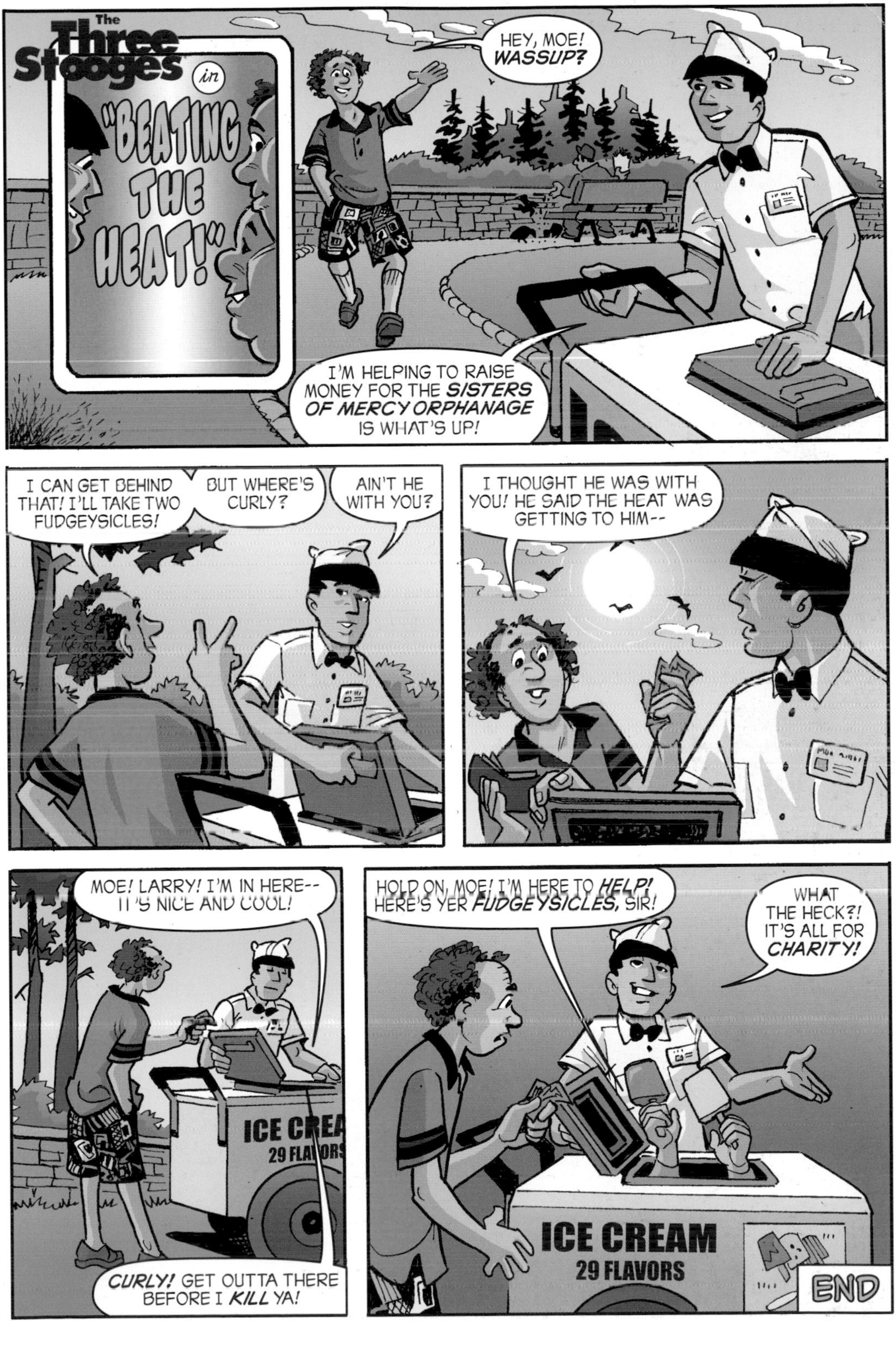

The Three Stooges in
"BEATING THE HEAT!"
HEY, MOE! WASSUP?
I'M HELPING TO RAISE MONEY FOR THE SISTERS OF MERCY ORPHANAGE IS WHAT'S UP!
I CAN GET BEHIND THAT! I'LL TAKE TWO FUDGEYSICLES!
BUT WHERE'S CURLY?
AIN'T HE WITH YOU?
I THOUGHT HE WAS WITH YOU! HE SAID THE HEAT WAS GETTING TO HIM--
MOE! LARRY! I'M IN HERE-- IT'S NICE AND COOL!
ICE CREAM
29 FLAVORS
CURLY! GET OUTTA THERE BEFORE I KILL YA!
HOLD ON, MOE! I'M HERE TO HELP! HERE'S YER FUDGEYSICLES, SIR!
WHAT THE HECK?! IT'S ALL FOR CHARITY!
ICE CREAM
29 FLAVORS
END

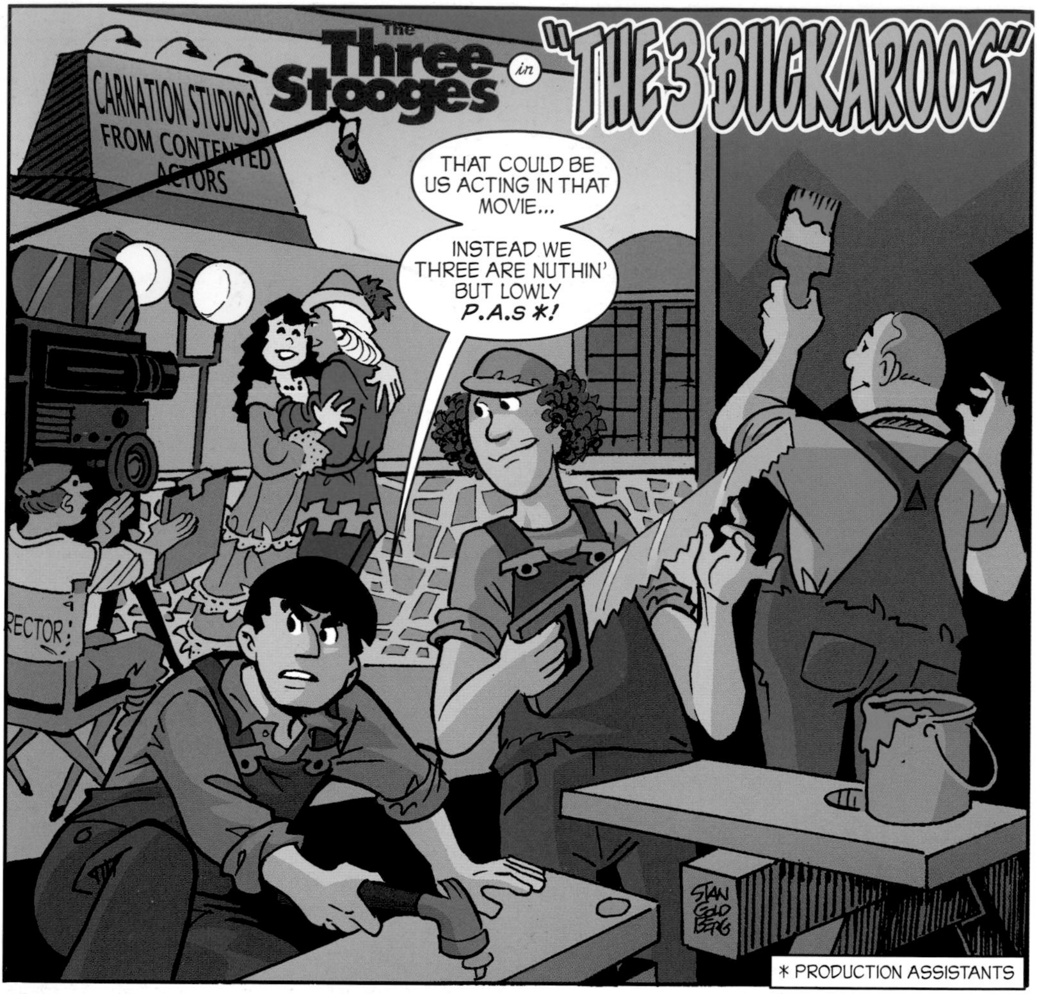
The Three Stooges in
"THE 3 BUCKAROOS"
CARNATION STUDIOS
FROM CONTENTED ACTORS
THAT COULD BE US ACTING IN THAT MOVIE...
INSTEAD WE THREE ARE NUTHIN' BUT LOWLY P.A.S *!
RECTOR
STAN GOLDBERG
* PRODUCTION ASSISTANTS

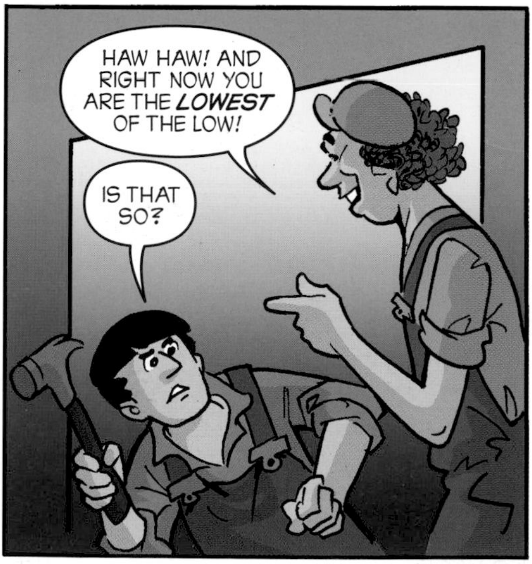
HAW HAW! AND RIGHT NOW YOU ARE THE LOWEST OF THE LOW!
IS THAT SO?

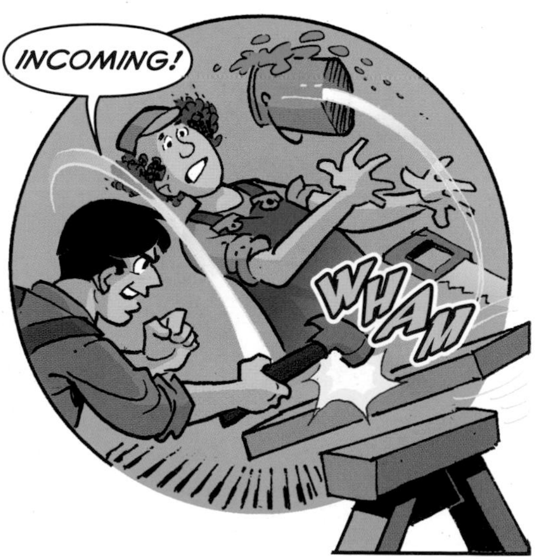
INCOMING!
WHAM

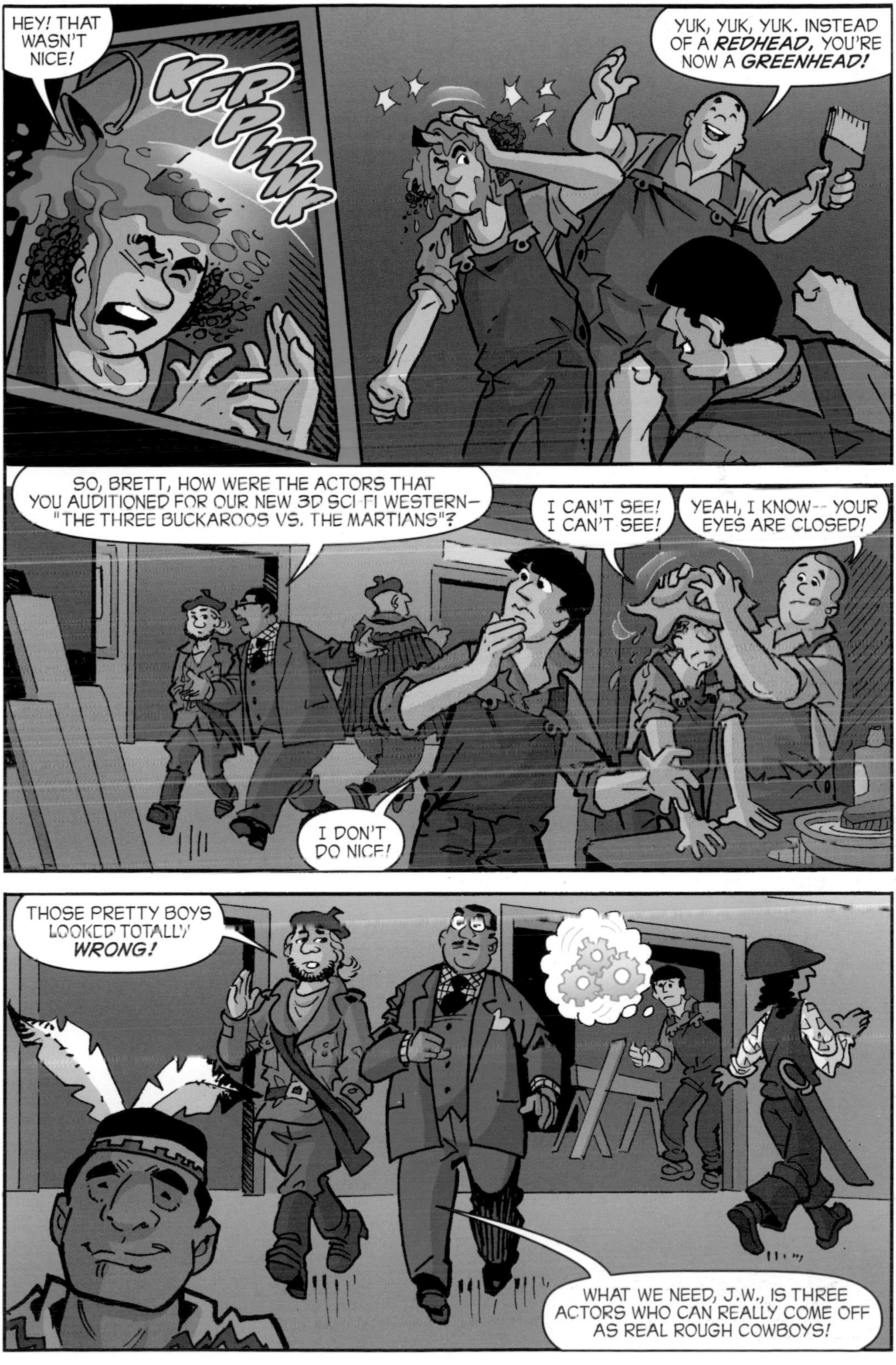
HEY! THAT WASN'T NICE!
KERPLUNK
YUK, YUK, YUK. INSTEAD OF A REDHEAD, YOU'RE NOW A GREENHEAD!
SO, BRETT, HOW WERE THE ACTORS THAT YOU AUDITIONED FOR OUR NEW 3D SCI-FI WESTERN— "THE THREE BUCKAROOS VS. THE MARTIANS"?
I CAN'T SEE! I CAN'T SEE!
YEAH, I KNOW-- YOUR EYES ARE CLOSED!
I DON'T DO NICE!
THOSE PRETTY BOYS LOOKED TOTALLY WRONG!
WHAT WE NEED, J.W., IS THREE ACTORS WHO CAN REALLY COME OFF AS REAL ROUGH COWBOYS!

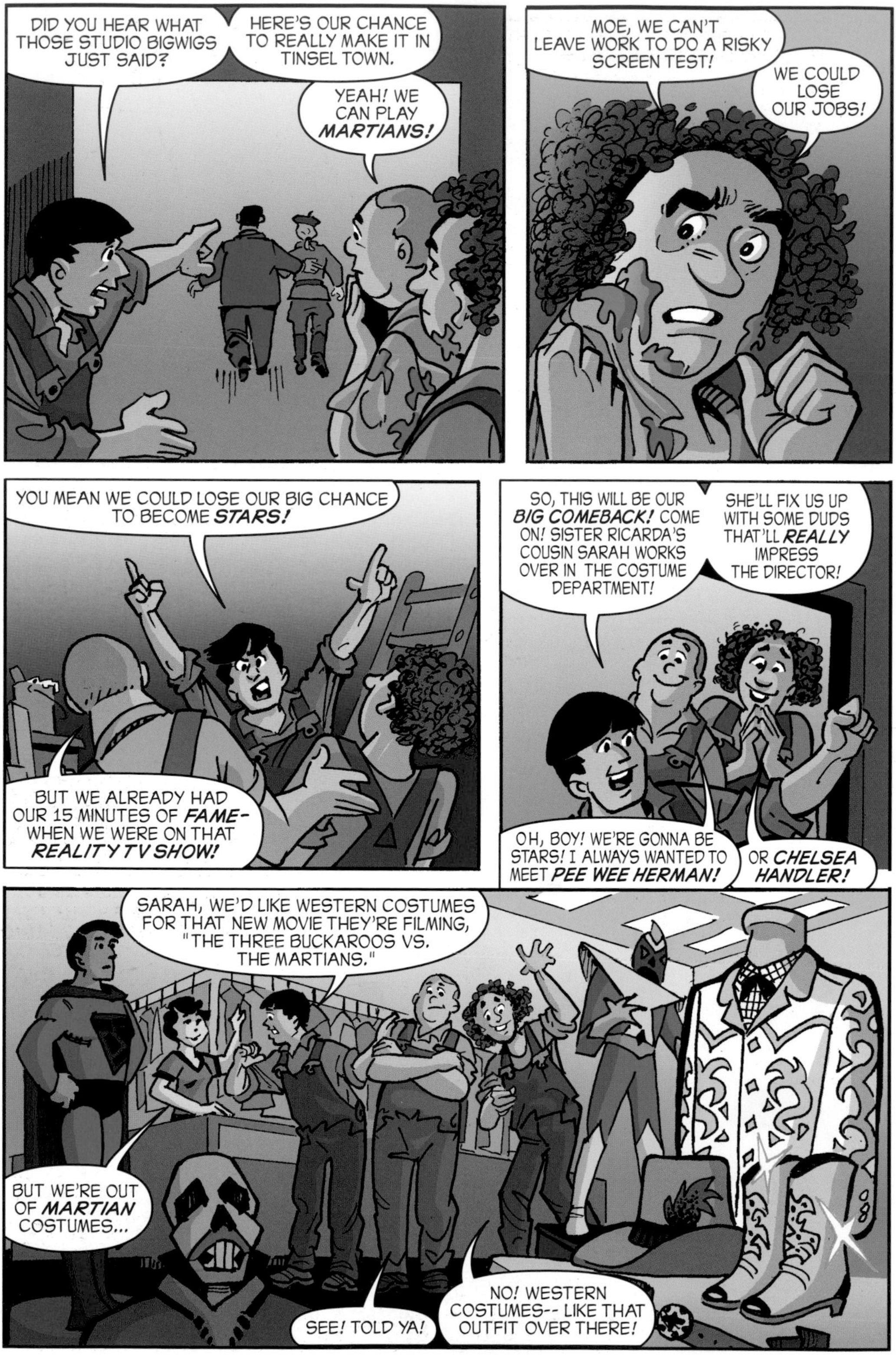
DID YOU HEAR WHAT THOSE STUDIO BIGWIGS JUST SAID?
HERE'S OUR CHANCE TO REALLY MAKE IT IN TINSEL TOWN.
YEAH! WE CAN PLAY MARTIANS!
MOE, WE CAN'T LEAVE WORK TO DO A RISKY SCREEN TEST!
WE COULD LOSE OUR JOBS!
YOU MEAN WE COULD LOSE OUR BIG CHANCE TO BECOME STARS!
BUT WE ALREADY HAD OUR 15 MINUTES OF FAME- WHEN WE WERE ON THAT REALITY TV SHOW!
SO, THIS WILL BE OUR BIG COMEBACK! COME ON! SISTER RICARDA'S COUSIN SARAH WORKS OVER IN THE COSTUME DEPARTMENT!
SHE'LL FIX US UP WITH SOME DUDS THAT'LL REALLY IMPRESS THE DIRECTOR!
OH, BOY! WE'RE GONNA BE STARS! I ALWAYS WANTED TO MEET PEE WEE HERMAN!
OR CHELSEA HANDLER!
SARAH, WE'D LIKE WESTERN COSTUMES FOR THAT NEW MOVIE THEY'RE FILMING, "THE THREE BUCKAROOS VS. THE MARTIANS."
BUT WE'RE OUT OF MARTIAN COSTUMES...
SEE! TOLD YA!
NO! WESTERN COSTUMES-- LIKE THAT OUTFIT OVER THERE!

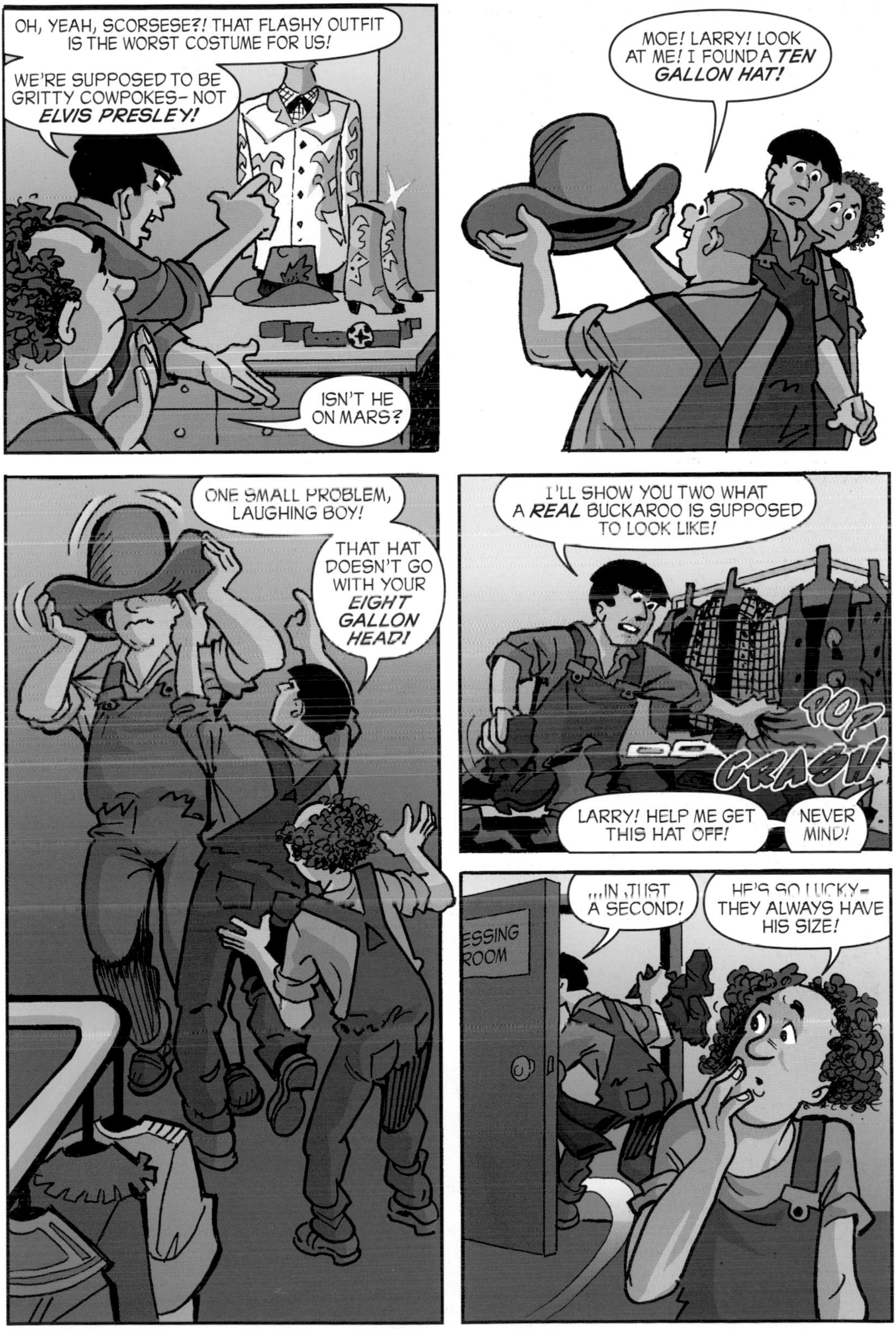

OH, YEAH, SCORSESE?! THAT FLASHY OUTFIT IS THE WORST COSTUME FOR US!
WE'RE SUPPOSED TO BE GRITTY COWPOKES– NOT ELVIS PRESLEY!
ISN'T HE ON MARS?
MOE! LARRY! LOOK AT ME! I FOUND A TEN GALLON HAT!
ONE SMALL PROBLEM, LAUGHING BOY!
THAT HAT DOESN'T GO WITH YOUR EIGHT GALLON HEAD!
I'LL SHOW YOU TWO WHAT A REAL BUCKAROO IS SUPPOSED TO LOOK LIKE!
POP
CRASH
LARRY! HELP ME GET THIS HAT OFF!
NEVER MIND!
...IN JUST A SECOND!
HE'S SO LUCKY– THEY ALWAYS HAVE HIS SIZE!
ESSING ROOM

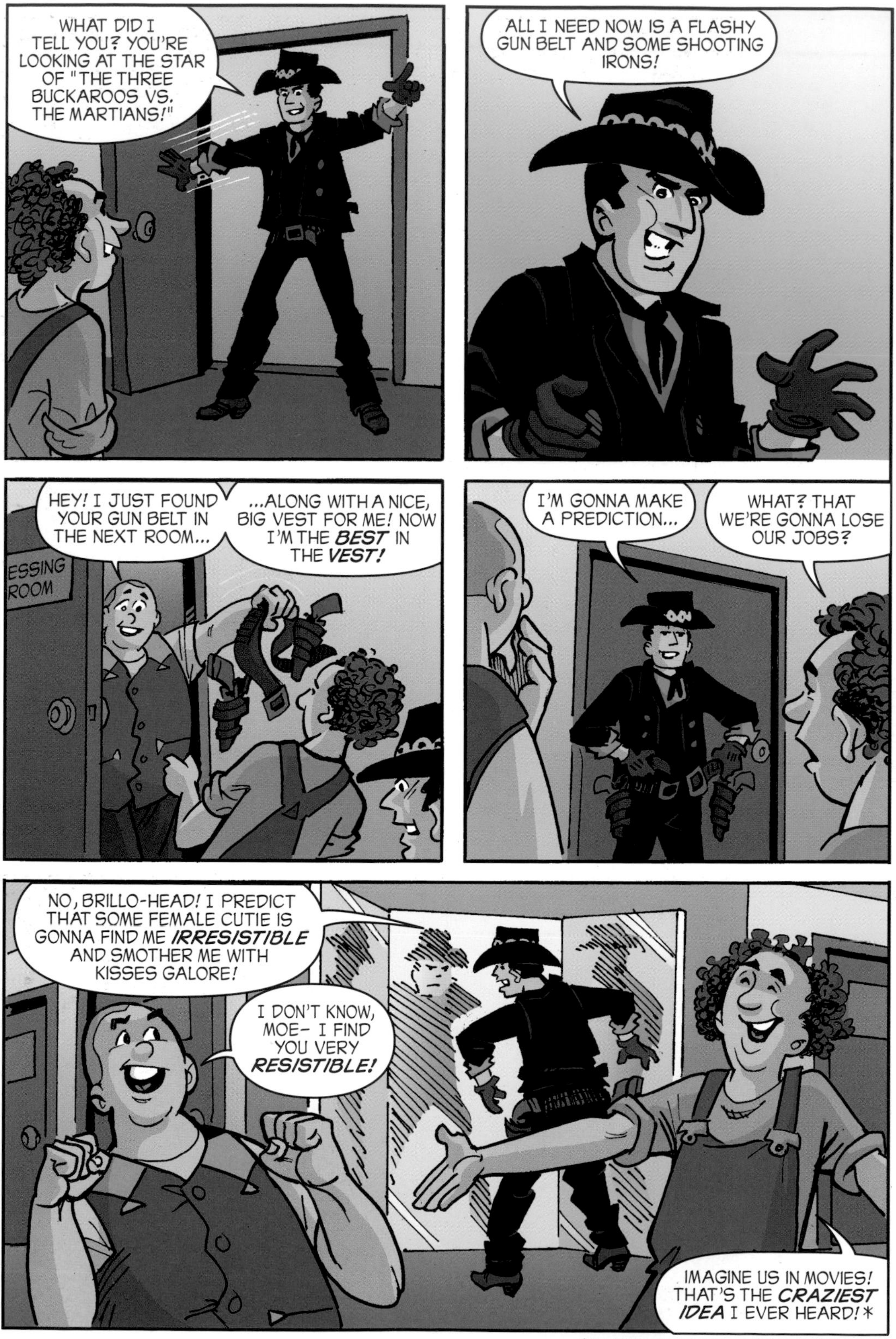
WHAT DID I TELL YOU? YOU'RE LOOKING AT THE STAR OF "THE THREE BUCKAROOS VS. THE MARTIANS!"
ALL I NEED NOW IS A FLASHY GUN BELT AND SOME SHOOTING IRONS!
HEY! I JUST FOUND YOUR GUN BELT IN THE NEXT ROOM...
...ALONG WITH A NICE, BIG VEST FOR ME! NOW I'M THE *BEST* IN THE *VEST!*
ESSING ROOM
I'M GONNA MAKE A PREDICTION...
WHAT? THAT WE'RE GONNA LOSE OUR JOBS?
NO, BRILLO-HEAD! I PREDICT THAT SOME FEMALE CUTIE IS GONNA FIND ME *IRRESISTIBLE* AND SMOTHER ME WITH KISSES GALORE!
I DON'T KNOW, MOE- I FIND YOU VERY *RESISTIBLE!*
IMAGINE US IN MOVIES! THAT'S THE *CRAZIEST IDEA* I EVER HEARD!*

**SHHH!* DON'T TELL 20TH CENTURY FOX!

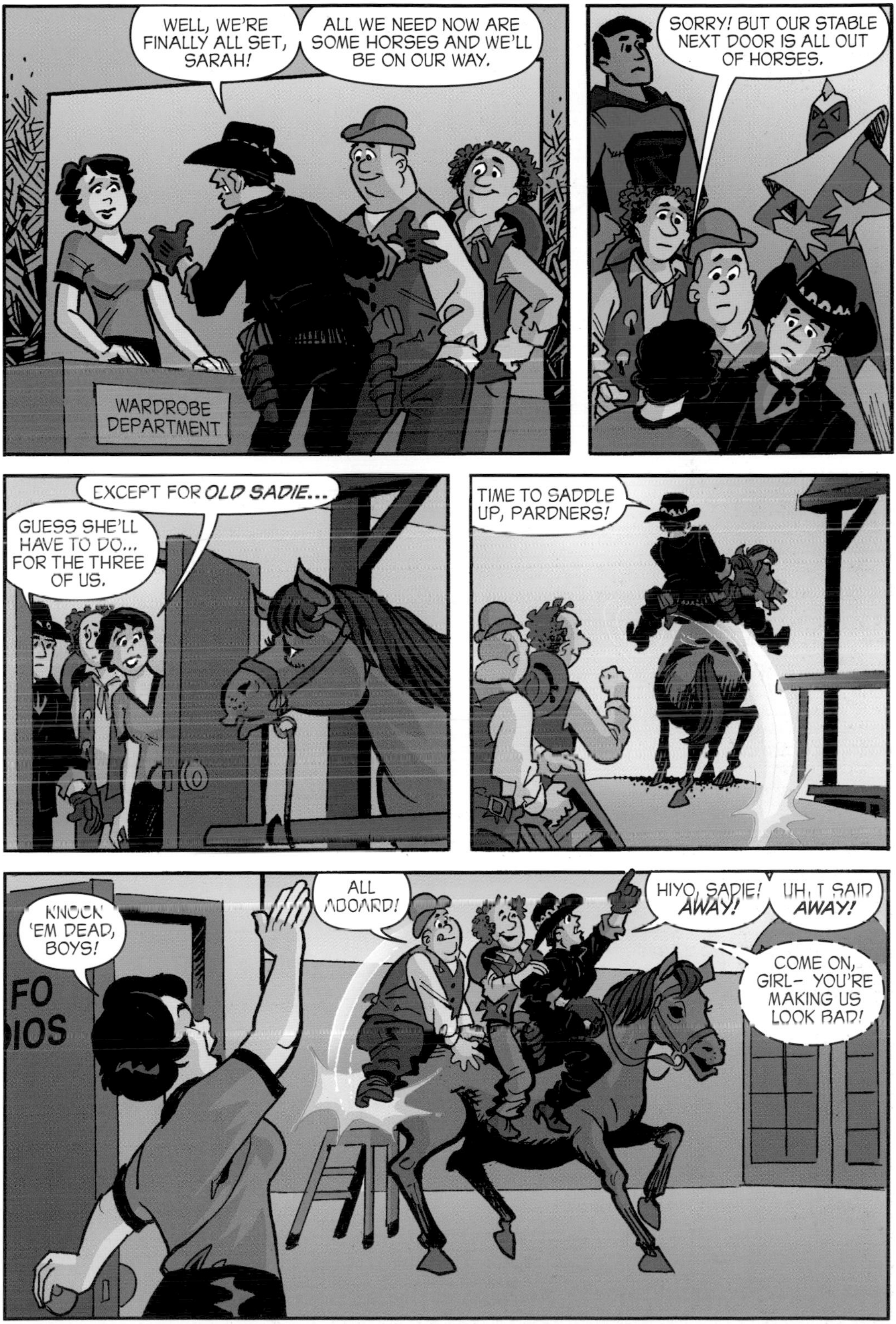
WELL, WE'RE FINALLY ALL SET, SARAH!
ALL WE NEED NOW ARE SOME HORSES AND WE'LL BE ON OUR WAY.
WARDROBE DEPARTMENT
SORRY! BUT OUR STABLE NEXT DOOR IS ALL OUT OF HORSES.
EXCEPT FOR *OLD SADIE*...
GUESS SHE'LL HAVE TO DO... FOR THE THREE OF US.
TIME TO SADDLE UP, PARDNERS!
KNOCK 'EM DEAD, BOYS!
ALL ABOARD!
HIYO, SADIE! **AWAY!**
UH, I SAID **AWAY!**
COME ON, GIRL- YOU'RE MAKING US LOOK BAD!

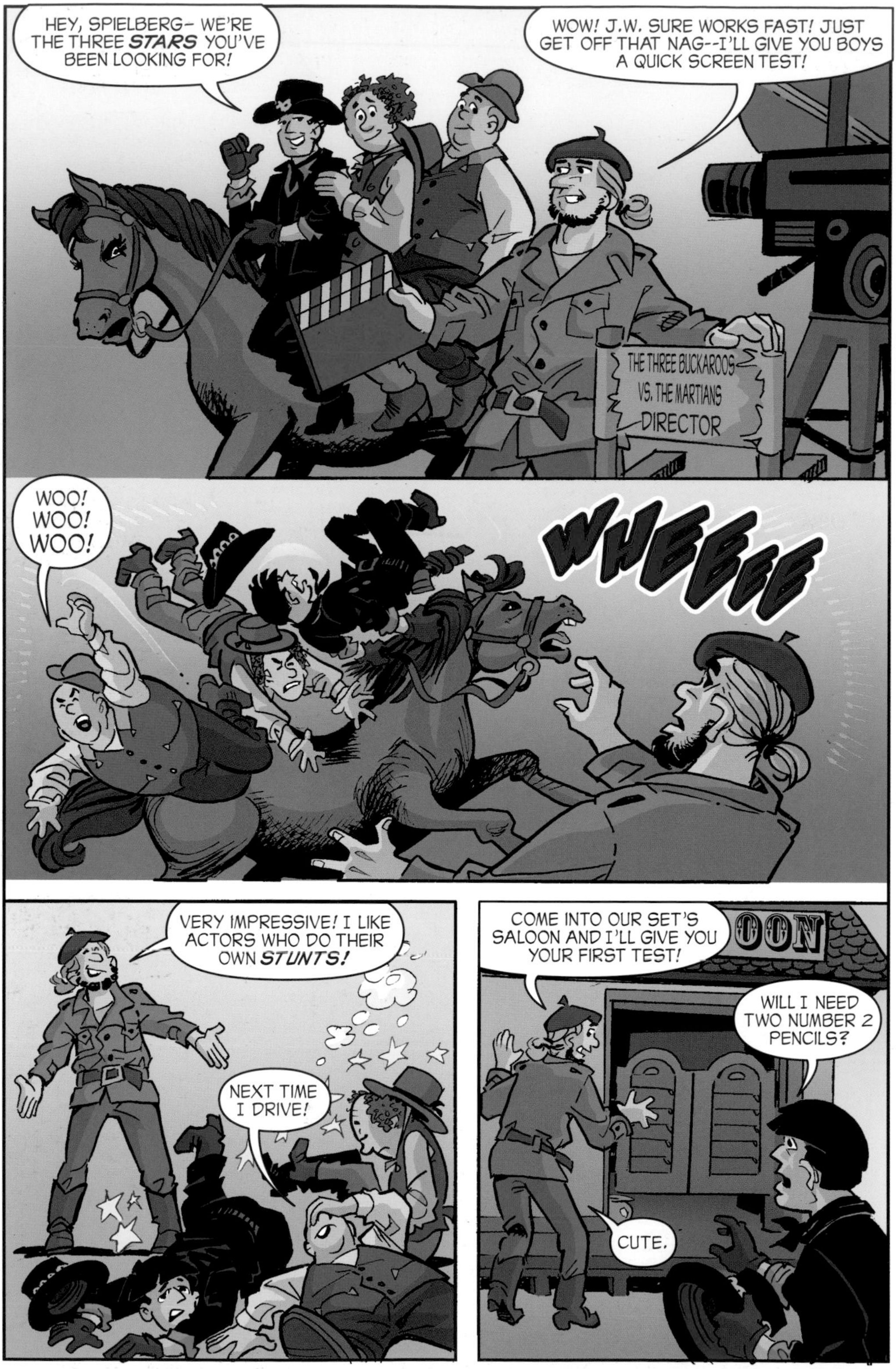
HEY, SPIELBERG– WE'RE THE THREE **STARS** YOU'VE BEEN LOOKING FOR!
WOW! J.W. SURE WORKS FAST! JUST GET OFF THAT NAG--I'LL GIVE YOU BOYS A QUICK SCREEN TEST!
THE THREE BUCKAROOS VS. THE MARTIANS DIRECTOR
WOO! WOO! WOO!
WHEEEE
VERY IMPRESSIVE! I LIKE ACTORS WHO DO THEIR OWN **STUNTS!**
NEXT TIME I DRIVE!
COME INTO OUR SET'S SALOON AND I'LL GIVE YOU YOUR FIRST TEST!
OON
WILL I NEED TWO NUMBER 2 PENCILS?
CUTE.

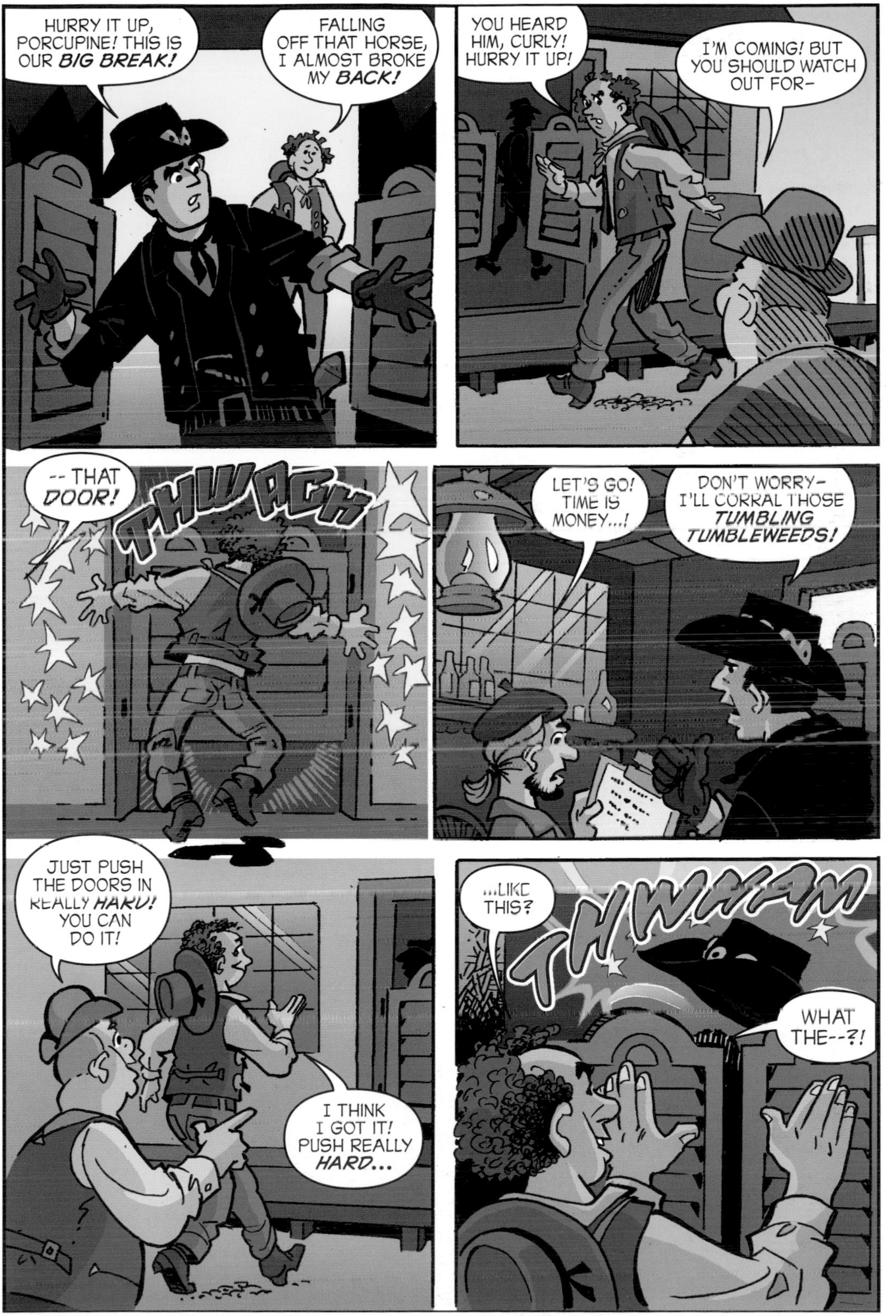
HURRY IT UP, PORCUPINE! THIS IS OUR BIG BREAK!
FALLING OFF THAT HORSE, I ALMOST BROKE MY BACK!
YOU HEARD HIM, CURLY! HURRY IT UP!
I'M COMING! BUT YOU SHOULD WATCH OUT FOR–
-- THAT DOOR!
THWACK
LET'S GO! TIME IS MONEY...!
DON'T WORRY– I'LL CORRAL THOSE TUMBLING TUMBLEWEEDS!
JUST PUSH THE DOORS IN REALLY HARD! YOU CAN DO IT!
I THINK I GOT IT! PUSH REALLY HARD...
...LIKE THIS?
THWAAAM
WHAT THE--?!

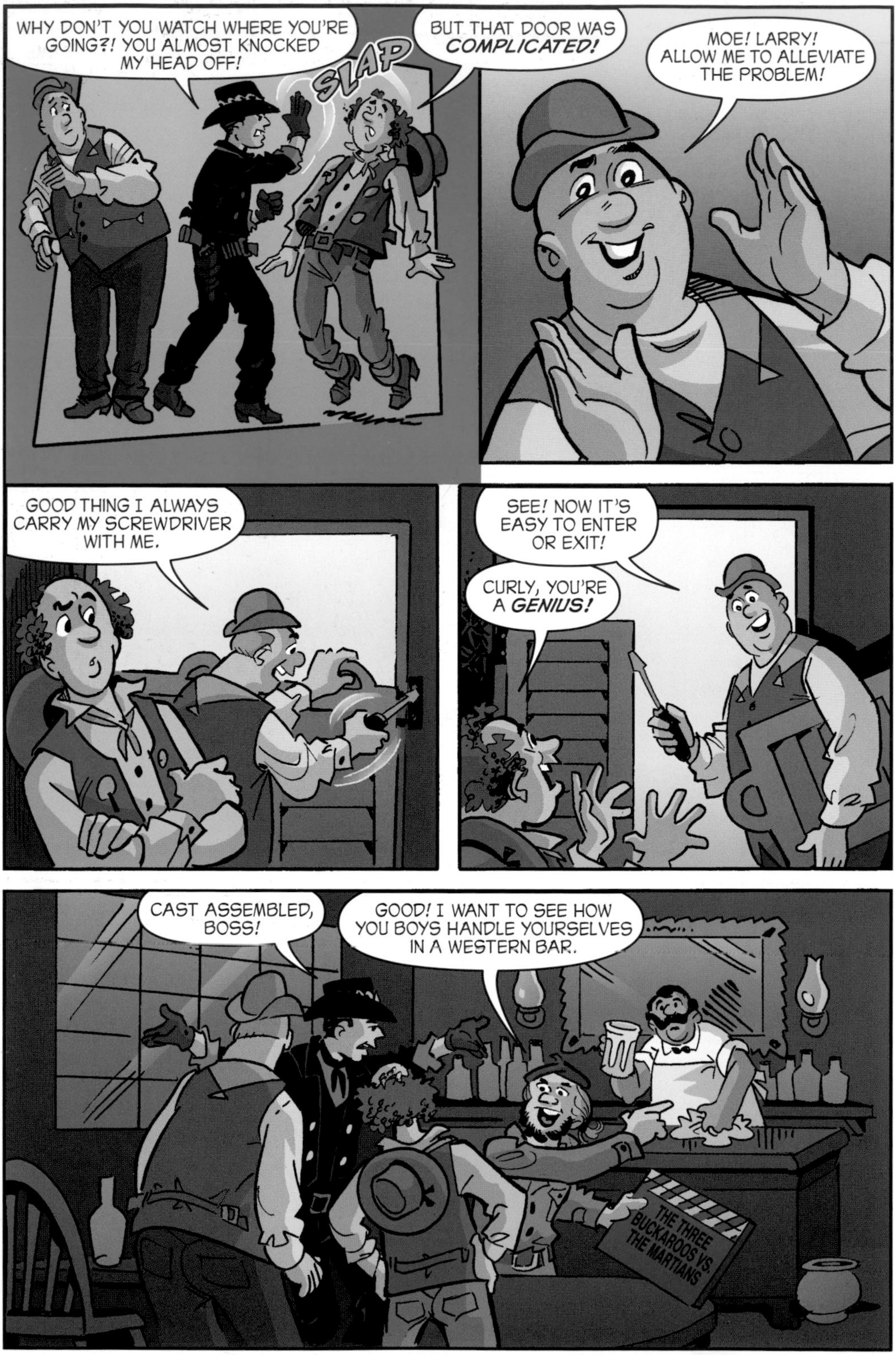
WHY DON'T YOU WATCH WHERE YOU'RE GOING?! YOU ALMOST KNOCKED MY HEAD OFF!
SLAP
BUT THAT DOOR WAS *COMPLICATED!*
MOE! LARRY! ALLOW ME TO ALLEVIATE THE PROBLEM!
GOOD THING I ALWAYS CARRY MY SCREWDRIVER WITH ME.
SEE! NOW IT'S EASY TO ENTER OR EXIT!
CURLY, YOU'RE A *GENIUS!*
CAST ASSEMBLED, BOSS!
GOOD! I WANT TO SEE HOW YOU BOYS HANDLE YOURSELVES IN A WESTERN BAR.
THE THREE BUCKAROOS VS. THE MARTIANS

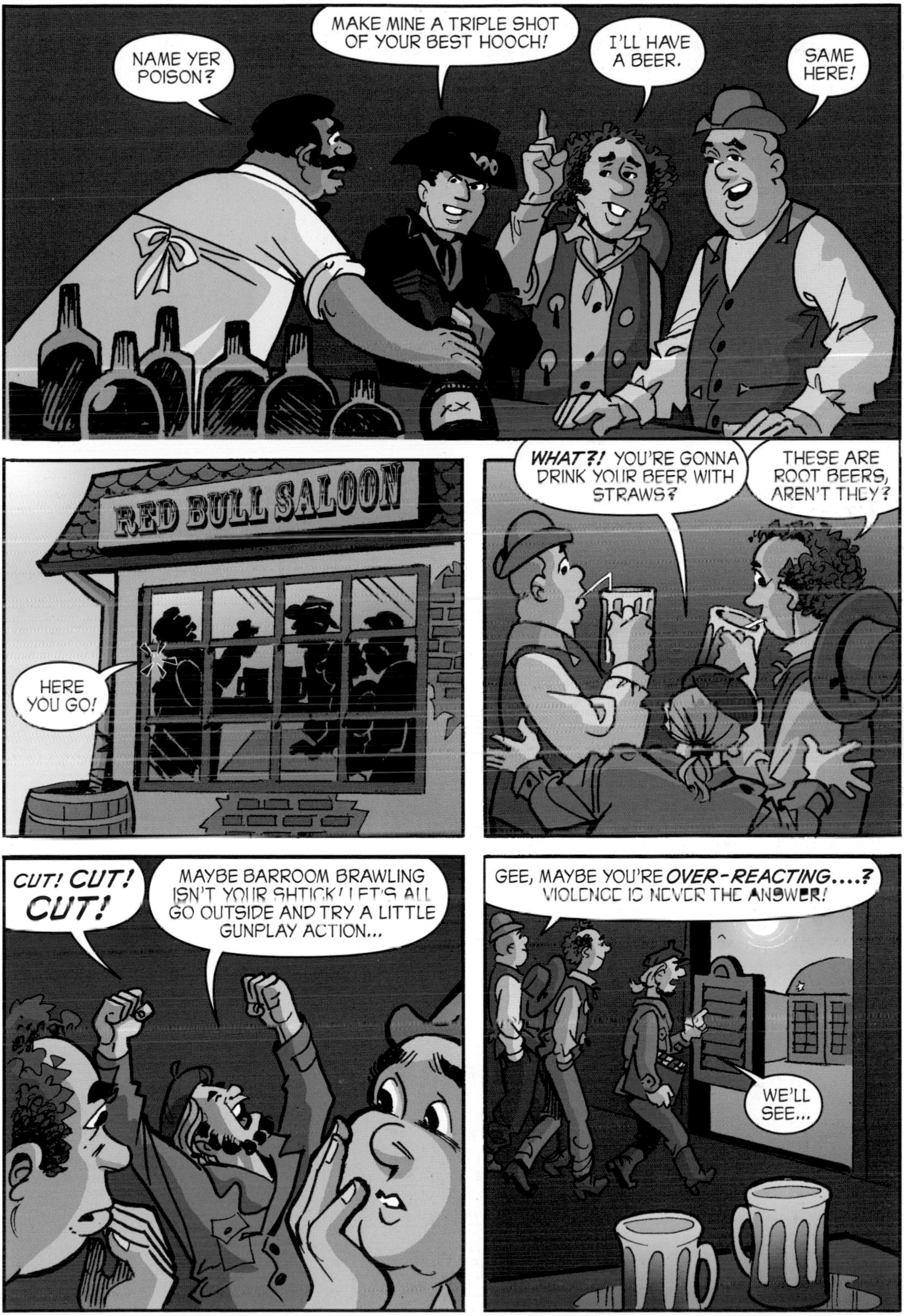
NAME YER POISON?
MAKE MINE A TRIPLE SHOT OF YOUR BEST HOOCH!
I'LL HAVE A BEER.
SAME HERE!
RED BULL SALOON
HERE YOU GO!
WHAT?! YOU'RE GONNA DRINK YOUR BEER WITH STRAWS?
THESE ARE ROOT BEERS, AREN'T THEY?
CUT! CUT! CUT!
MAYBE BARROOM BRAWLING ISN'T YOUR SHTICK! LET'S ALL GO OUTSIDE AND TRY A LITTLE GUNPLAY ACTION...
GEE, MAYBE YOU'RE OVER-REACTING....? VIOLENCE IS NEVER THE ANSWER!
WE'LL SEE...

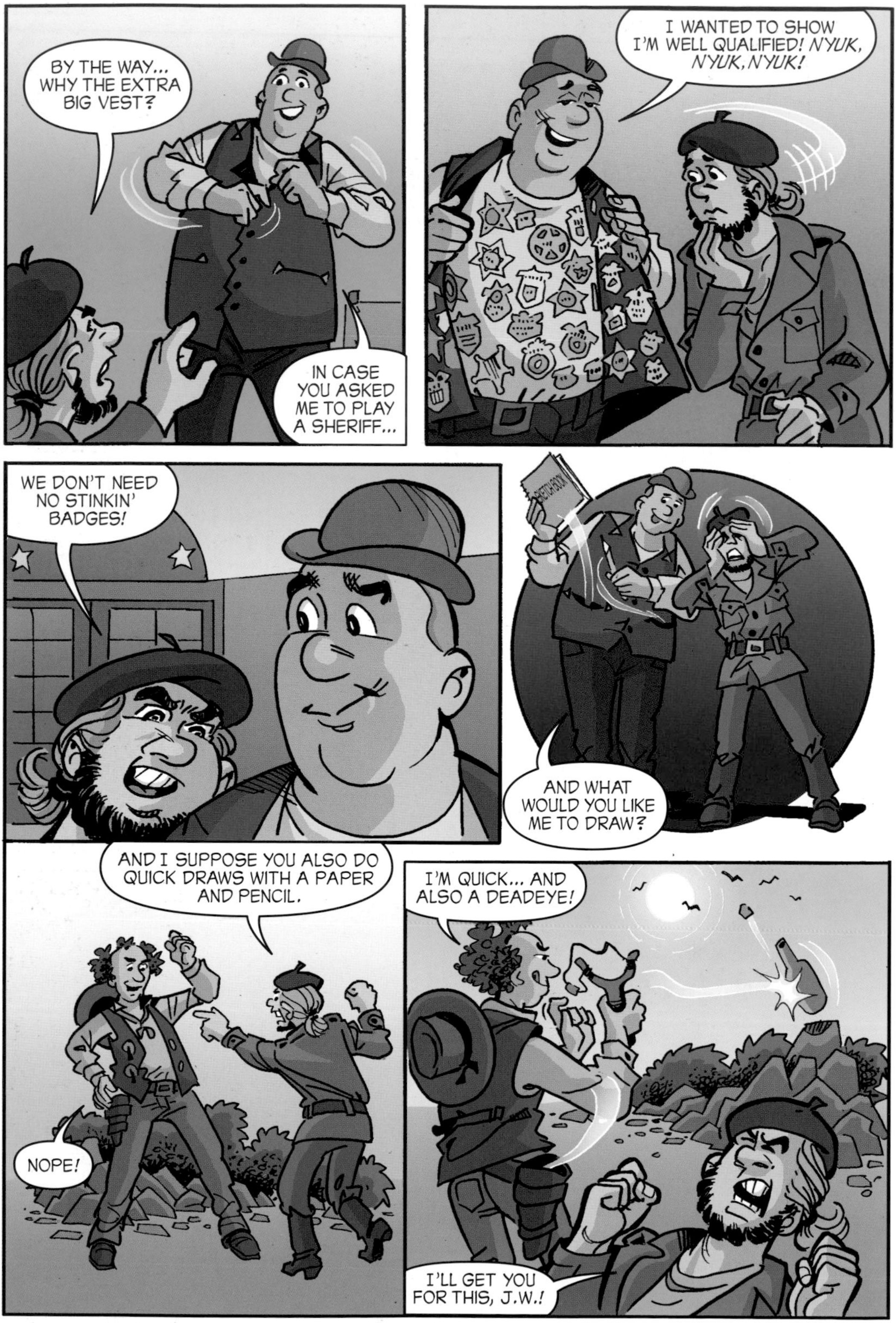
BY THE WAY... WHY THE EXTRA BIG VEST?
IN CASE YOU ASKED ME TO PLAY A SHERIFF...
I WANTED TO SHOW I'M WELL QUALIFIED! *NYUK, NYUK, NYUK!*
WE DON'T NEED NO STINKIN' BADGES!
SKETCHBOOK
AND WHAT WOULD YOU LIKE ME TO DRAW?
AND I SUPPOSE YOU ALSO DO QUICK DRAWS WITH A PAPER AND PENCIL.
NOPE!
I'M QUICK... AND ALSO A DEADEYE!
I'LL GET YOU FOR THIS, J.W.!

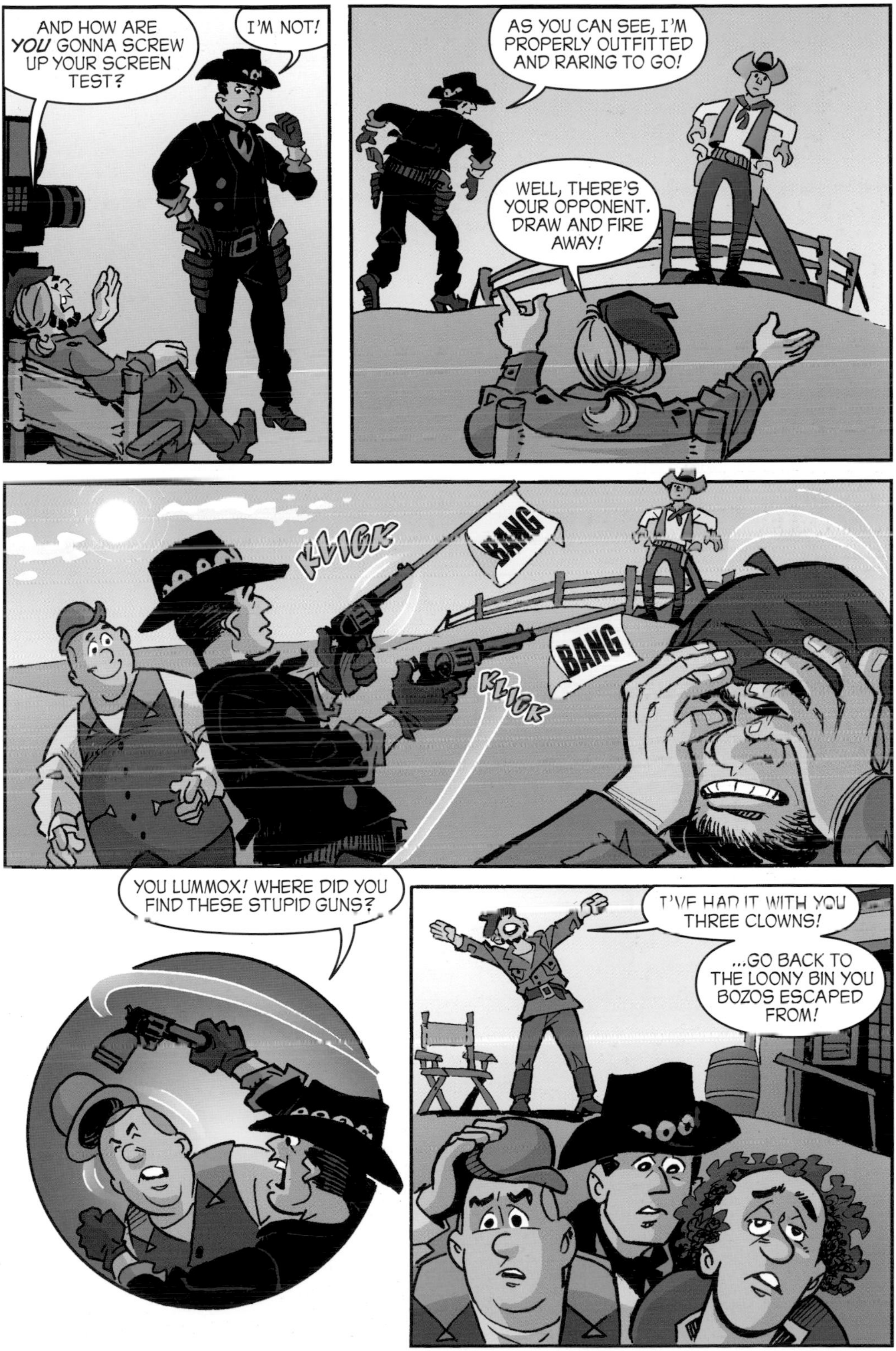
AND HOW ARE YOU GONNA SCREW UP YOUR SCREEN TEST?
I'M NOT!
AS YOU CAN SEE, I'M PROPERLY OUTFITTED AND RARING TO GO!
WELL, THERE'S YOUR OPPONENT. DRAW AND FIRE AWAY!
KLICK
BANG
BANG
KLICK
YOU LUMMOX! WHERE DID YOU FIND THESE STUPID GUNS?
I'VE HAD IT WITH YOU THREE CLOWNS!
...GO BACK TO THE LOONY BIN YOU BOZOS ESCAPED FROM!

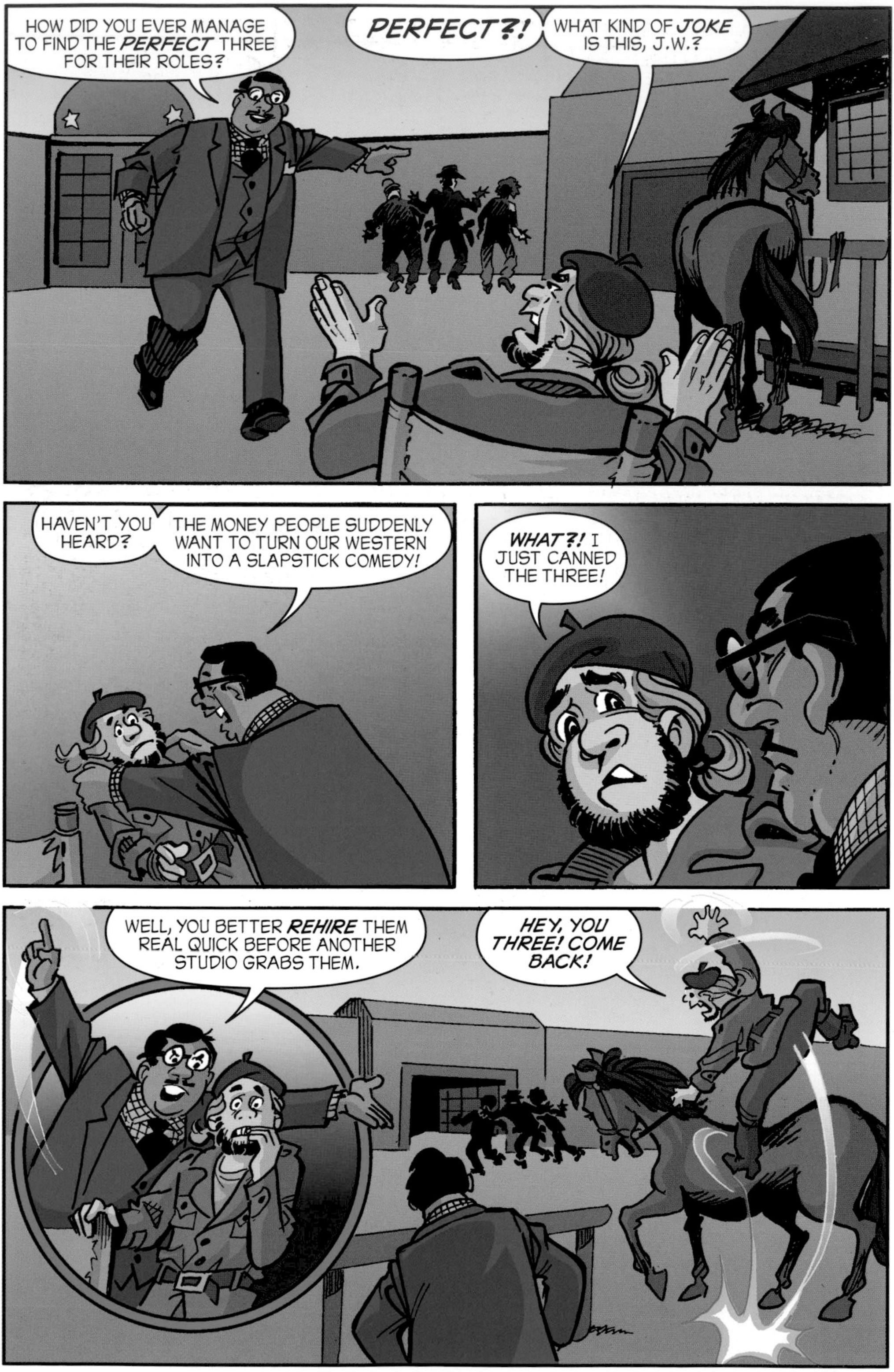
HOW DID YOU EVER MANAGE TO FIND THE *PERFECT* THREE FOR THEIR ROLES?
PERFECT?!
WHAT KIND OF *JOKE* IS THIS, J.W.?
HAVEN'T YOU HEARD?
THE MONEY PEOPLE SUDDENLY WANT TO TURN OUR WESTERN INTO A SLAPSTICK COMEDY!
WHAT?! I JUST CANNED THE THREE!
WELL, YOU BETTER *REHIRE* THEM REAL QUICK BEFORE ANOTHER STUDIO GRABS THEM.
HEY, YOU THREE! COME BACK!

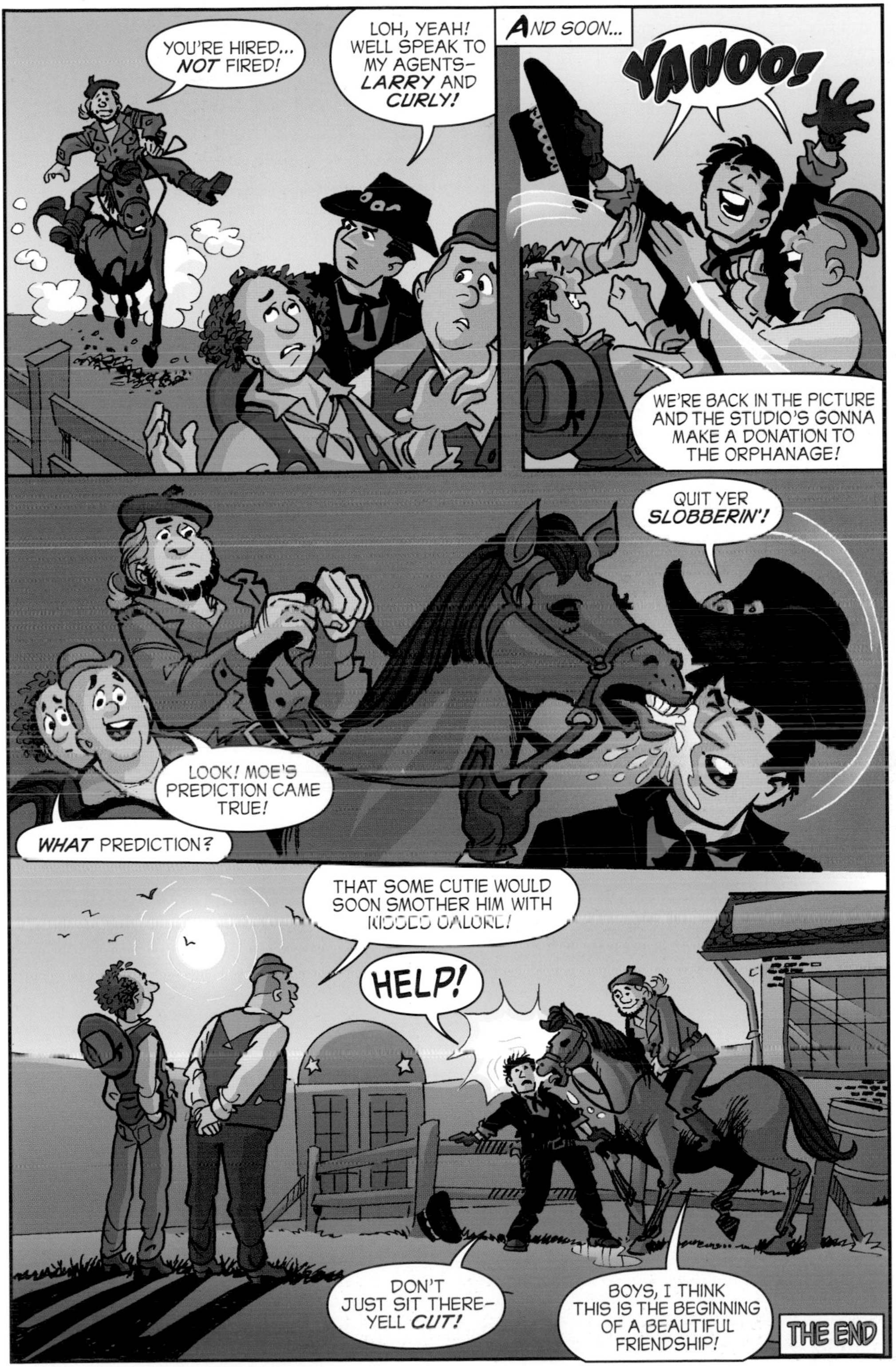
YOU'RE HIRED... NOT FIRED!
LOH, YEAH! WELL SPEAK TO MY AGENTS- LARRY AND CURLY!
AND SOON...
YAHOO!
WE'RE BACK IN THE PICTURE AND THE STUDIO'S GONNA MAKE A DONATION TO THE ORPHANAGE!
QUIT YER SLOBBERIN'!
LOOK! MOE'S PREDICTION CAME TRUE!
WHAT PREDICTION?
THAT SOME CUTIE WOULD SOON SMOTHER HIM WITH KISSES GALORE!
HELP!
DON'T JUST SIT THERE- YELL CUT!
BOYS, I THINK THIS IS THE BEGINNING OF A BEAUTIFUL FRIENDSHIP!
THE END

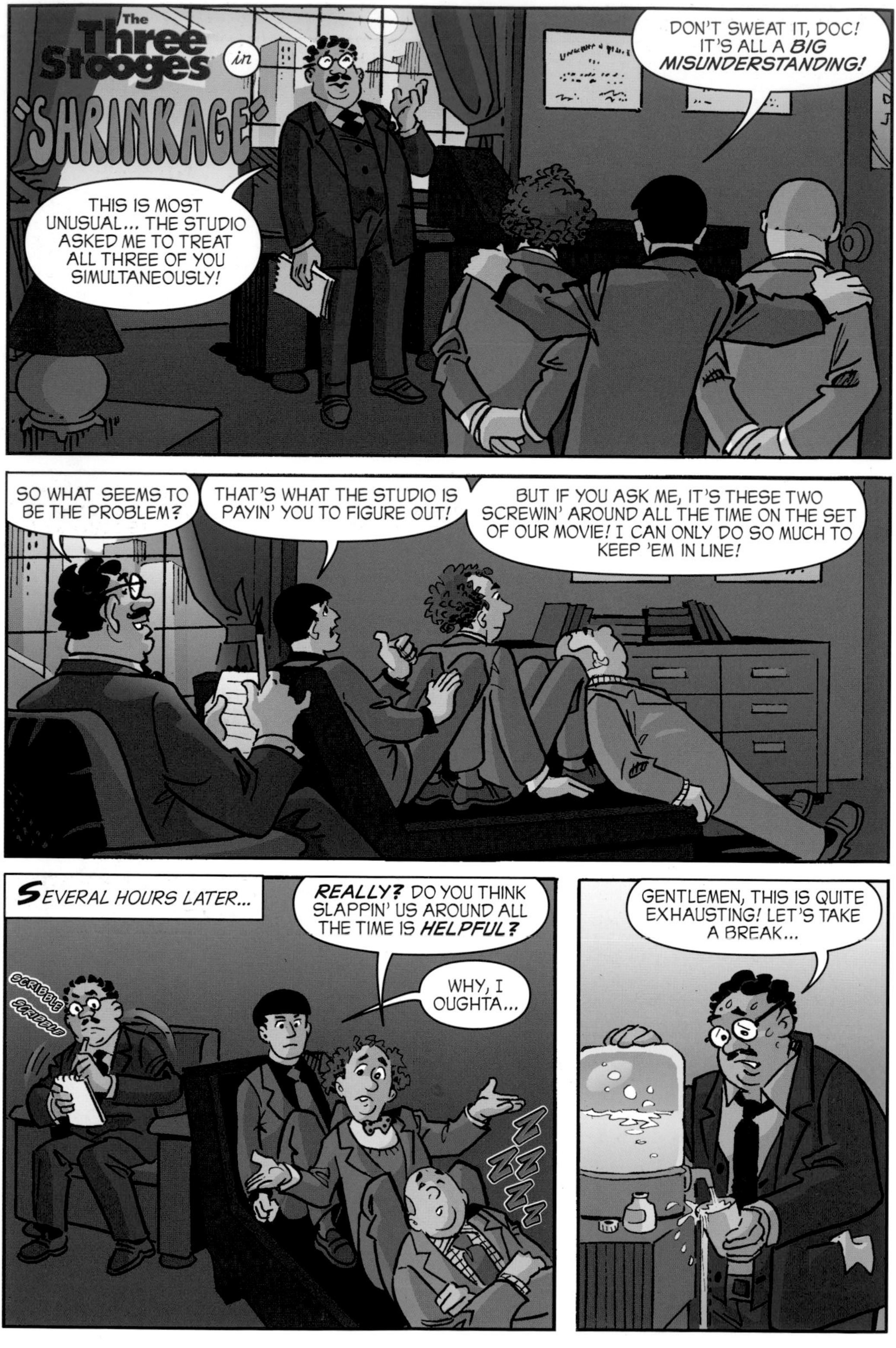
The Three Stooges in
"SHRINKAGE"
THIS IS MOST UNUSUAL... THE STUDIO ASKED ME TO TREAT ALL THREE OF YOU SIMULTANEOUSLY!
DON'T SWEAT IT, DOC! IT'S ALL A *BIG MISUNDERSTANDING!*
SO WHAT SEEMS TO BE THE PROBLEM?
THAT'S WHAT THE STUDIO IS PAYIN' YOU TO FIGURE OUT!
BUT IF YOU ASK ME, IT'S THESE TWO SCREWIN' AROUND ALL THE TIME ON THE SET OF OUR MOVIE! I CAN ONLY DO SO MUCH TO KEEP 'EM IN LINE!
SEVERAL HOURS LATER...
SCRIBBLE SCRIBBLE
REALLY? DO YOU THINK SLAPPIN' US AROUND ALL THE TIME IS *HELPFUL?*
WHY, I OUGHTA...
ZZZZ
GENTLEMEN, THIS IS QUITE EXHAUSTING! LET'S TAKE A BREAK...

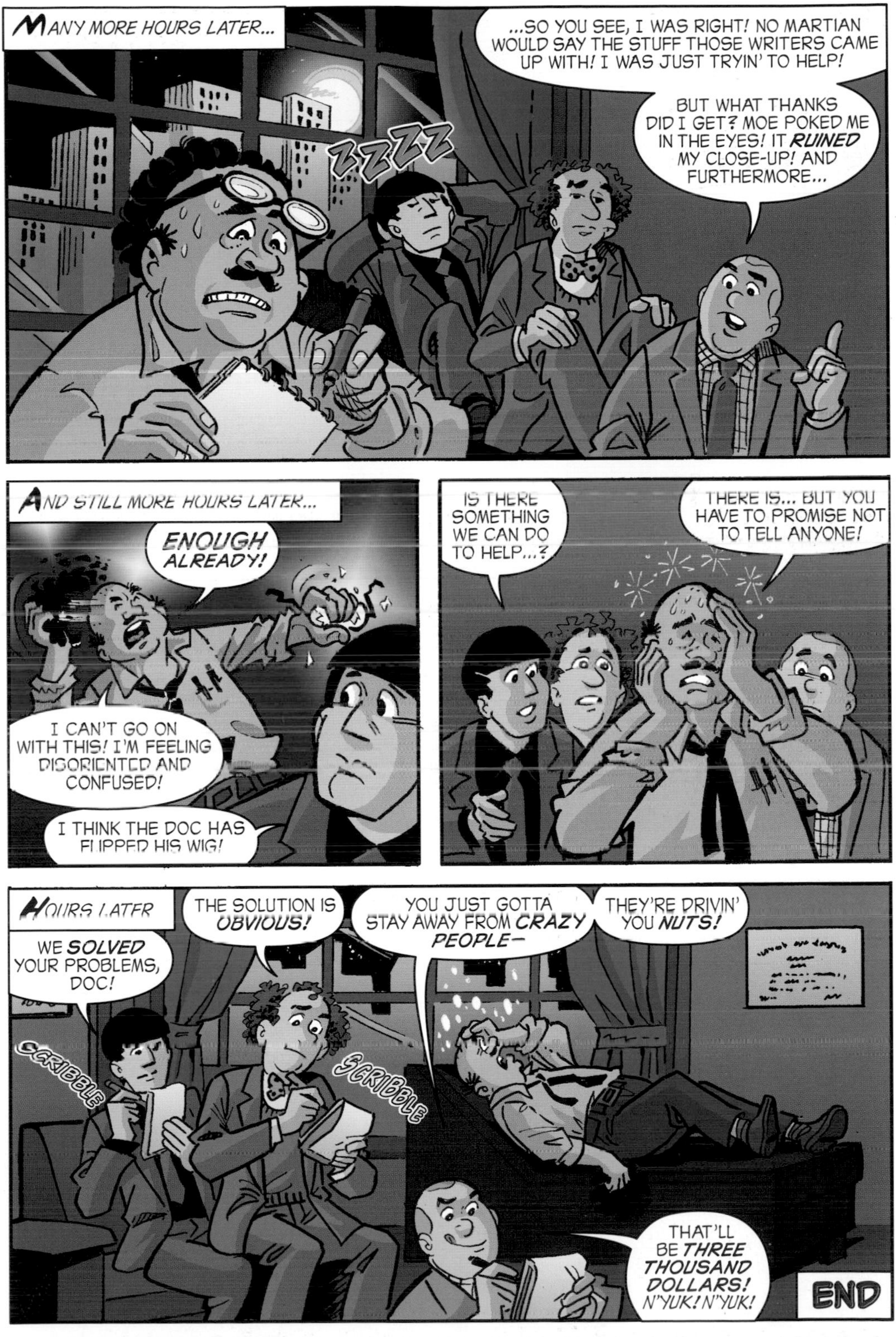
MANY MORE HOURS LATER...
...SO YOU SEE, I WAS RIGHT! NO MARTIAN WOULD SAY THE STUFF THOSE WRITERS CAME UP WITH! I WAS JUST TRYIN' TO HELP!
BUT WHAT THANKS DID I GET? MOE POKED ME IN THE EYES! IT RUINED MY CLOSE-UP! AND FURTHERMORE...
ZZZZ
AND STILL MORE HOURS LATER...
ENOUGH ALREADY!
I CAN'T GO ON WITH THIS! I'M FEELING DISORIENTED AND CONFUSED!
I THINK THE DOC HAS FLIPPED HIS WIG!
IS THERE SOMETHING WE CAN DO TO HELP...?
THERE IS... BUT YOU HAVE TO PROMISE NOT TO TELL ANYONE!
HOURS LATER
WE SOLVED YOUR PROBLEMS, DOC!
THE SOLUTION IS OBVIOUS!
YOU JUST GOTTA STAY AWAY FROM CRAZY PEOPLE—
THEY'RE DRIVIN' YOU NUTS!
SCRIBBLE
SCRIBBLE
THAT'LL BE THREE THOUSAND DOLLARS! N'YUK! N'YUK!
END

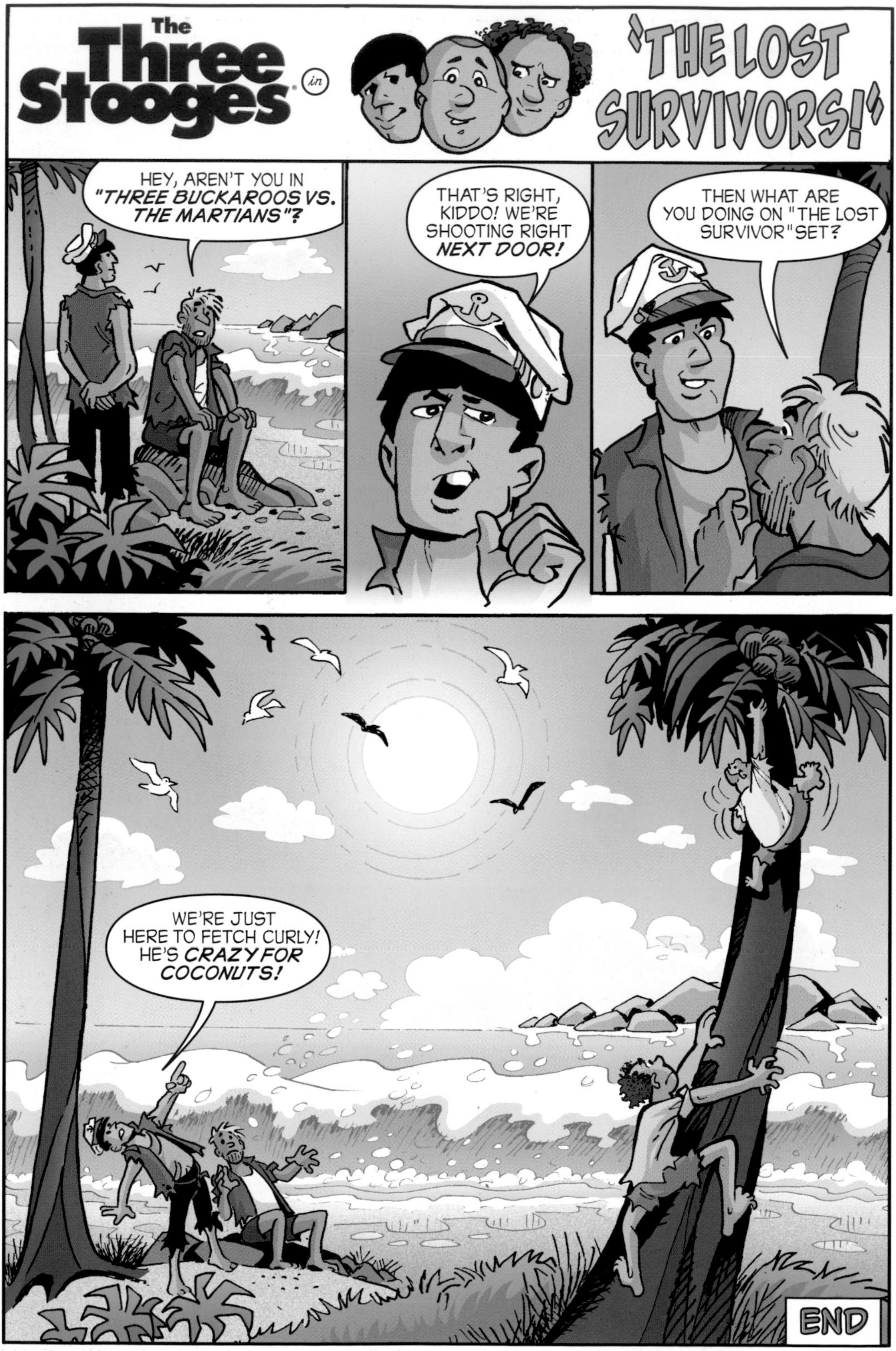
The Three Stooges in
"THE LOST SURVIVORS!"
HEY, AREN'T YOU IN "THREE BUCKAROOS VS. THE MARTIANS"?
THAT'S RIGHT, KIDDO! WE'RE SHOOTING RIGHT NEXT DOOR!
THEN WHAT ARE YOU DOING ON "THE LOST SURVIVOR" SET?
WE'RE JUST HERE TO FETCH CURLY! HE'S CRAZY FOR COCONUTS!
END

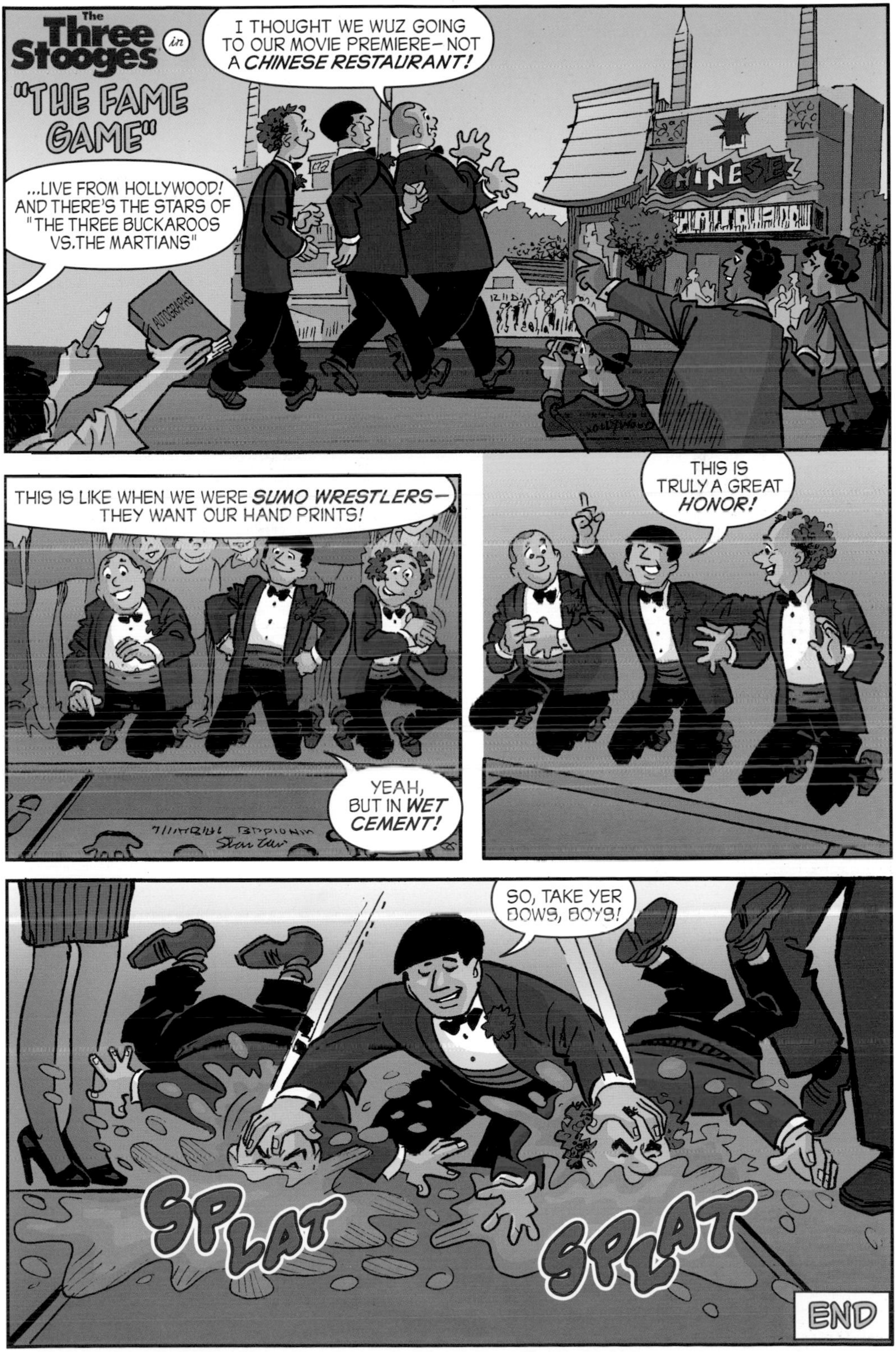
The Three Stooges in
"THE FAME GAME"
I THOUGHT WE WUZ GOING TO OUR MOVIE PREMIERE– NOT A CHINESE RESTAURANT!
...LIVE FROM HOLLYWOOD! AND THERE'S THE STARS OF "THE THREE BUCKAROOS VS.THE MARTIANS"
AUTOGRAPHS
CHINESE
THIS IS LIKE WHEN WE WERE SUMO WRESTLERS– THEY WANT OUR HAND PRINTS!
YEAH, BUT IN WET CEMENT!
THIS IS TRULY A GREAT HONOR!
SO, TAKE YER BOWS, BOYS!
SPLAT
SPLAT
END

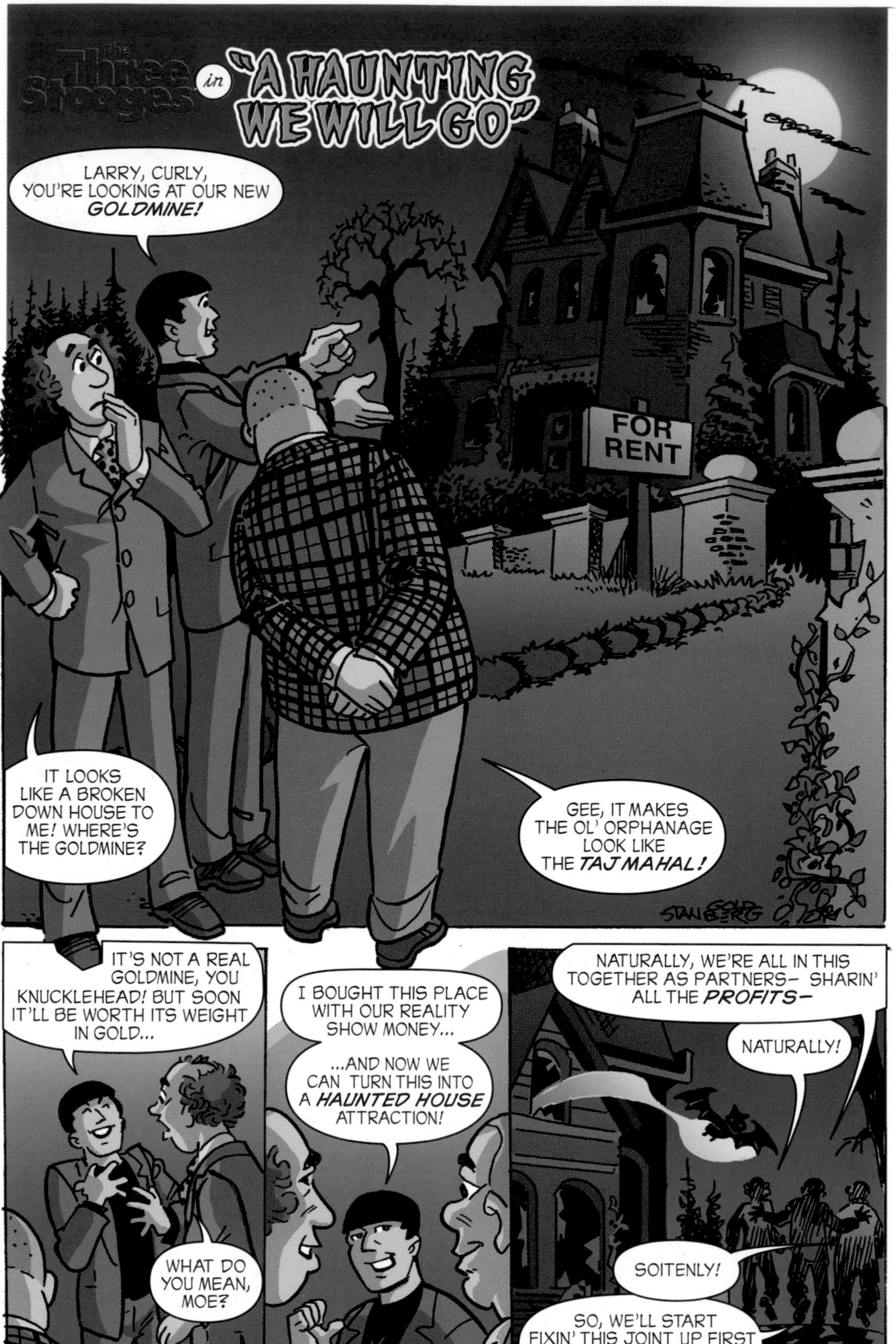
The Three Stooges in "A HAUNTING WE WILL GO"
LARRY, CURLY, YOU'RE LOOKING AT OUR NEW GOLDMINE!
FOR RENT
IT LOOKS LIKE A BROKEN DOWN HOUSE TO ME! WHERE'S THE GOLDMINE?
GEE, IT MAKES THE OL' ORPHANAGE LOOK LIKE THE TAJ MAHAL!
IT'S NOT A REAL GOLDMINE, YOU KNUCKLEHEAD! BUT SOON IT'LL BE WORTH ITS WEIGHT IN GOLD...
WHAT DO YOU MEAN, MOE?
I BOUGHT THIS PLACE WITH OUR REALITY SHOW MONEY...
...AND NOW WE CAN TURN THIS INTO A HAUNTED HOUSE ATTRACTION!
NATURALLY, WE'RE ALL IN THIS TOGETHER AS PARTNERS— SHARIN' ALL THE PROFITS—
NATURALLY!
SOITENLY!
SO, WE'LL START FIXIN' THIS JOINT UP FIRST THING TOMORROW!

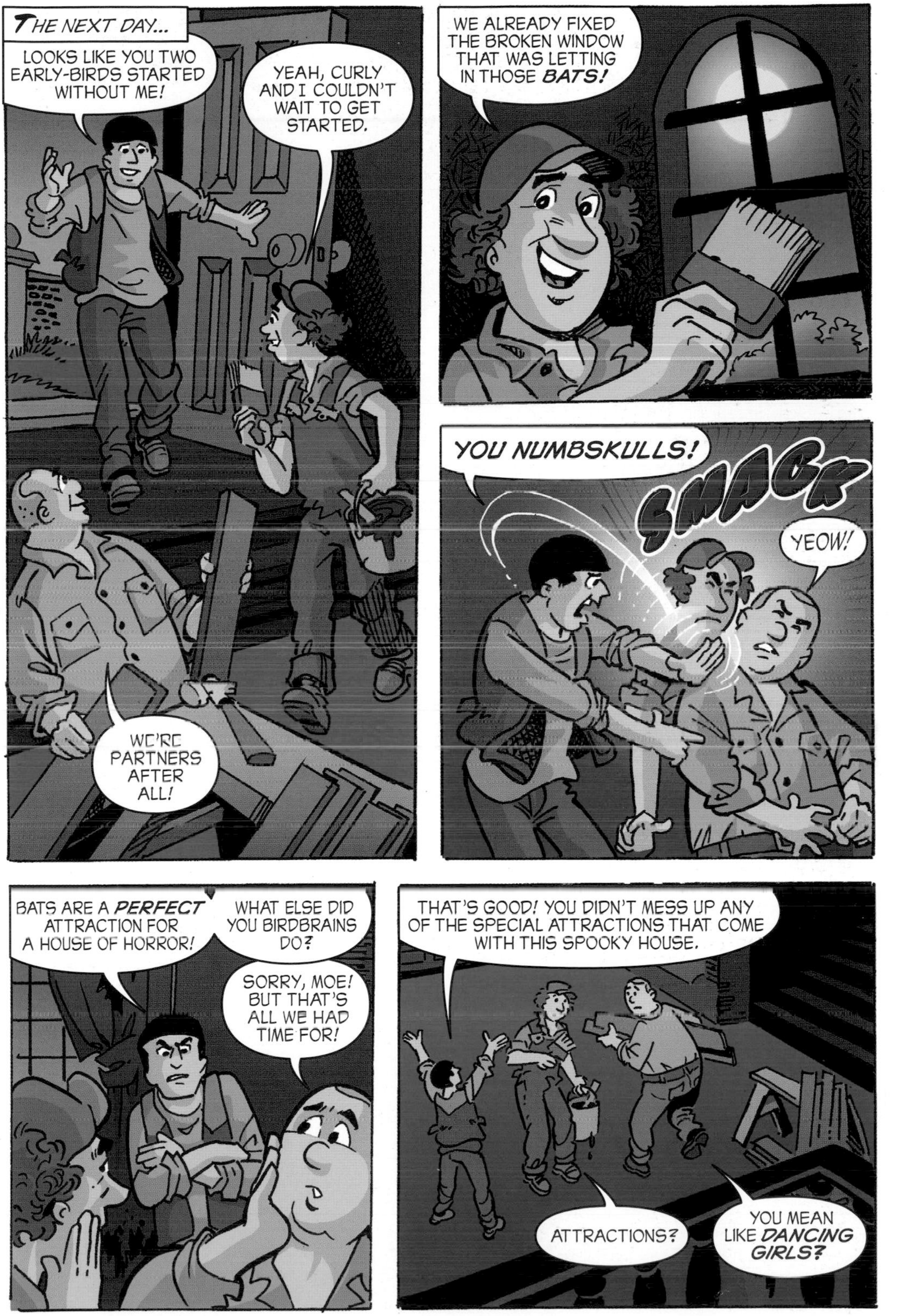
THE NEXT DAY...
LOOKS LIKE YOU TWO EARLY-BIRDS STARTED WITHOUT ME!
YEAH, CURLY AND I COULDN'T WAIT TO GET STARTED.
WE'RE PARTNERS AFTER ALL!
WE ALREADY FIXED THE BROKEN WINDOW THAT WAS LETTING IN THOSE BATS!
YOU NUMBSKULLS!
SMACK
YEOW!
BATS ARE A PERFECT ATTRACTION FOR A HOUSE OF HORROR!
WHAT ELSE DID YOU BIRDBRAINS DO?
SORRY, MOE! BUT THAT'S ALL WE HAD TIME FOR!
THAT'S GOOD! YOU DIDN'T MESS UP ANY OF THE SPECIAL ATTRACTIONS THAT COME WITH THIS SPOOKY HOUSE.
ATTRACTIONS?
YOU MEAN LIKE DANCING GIRLS?

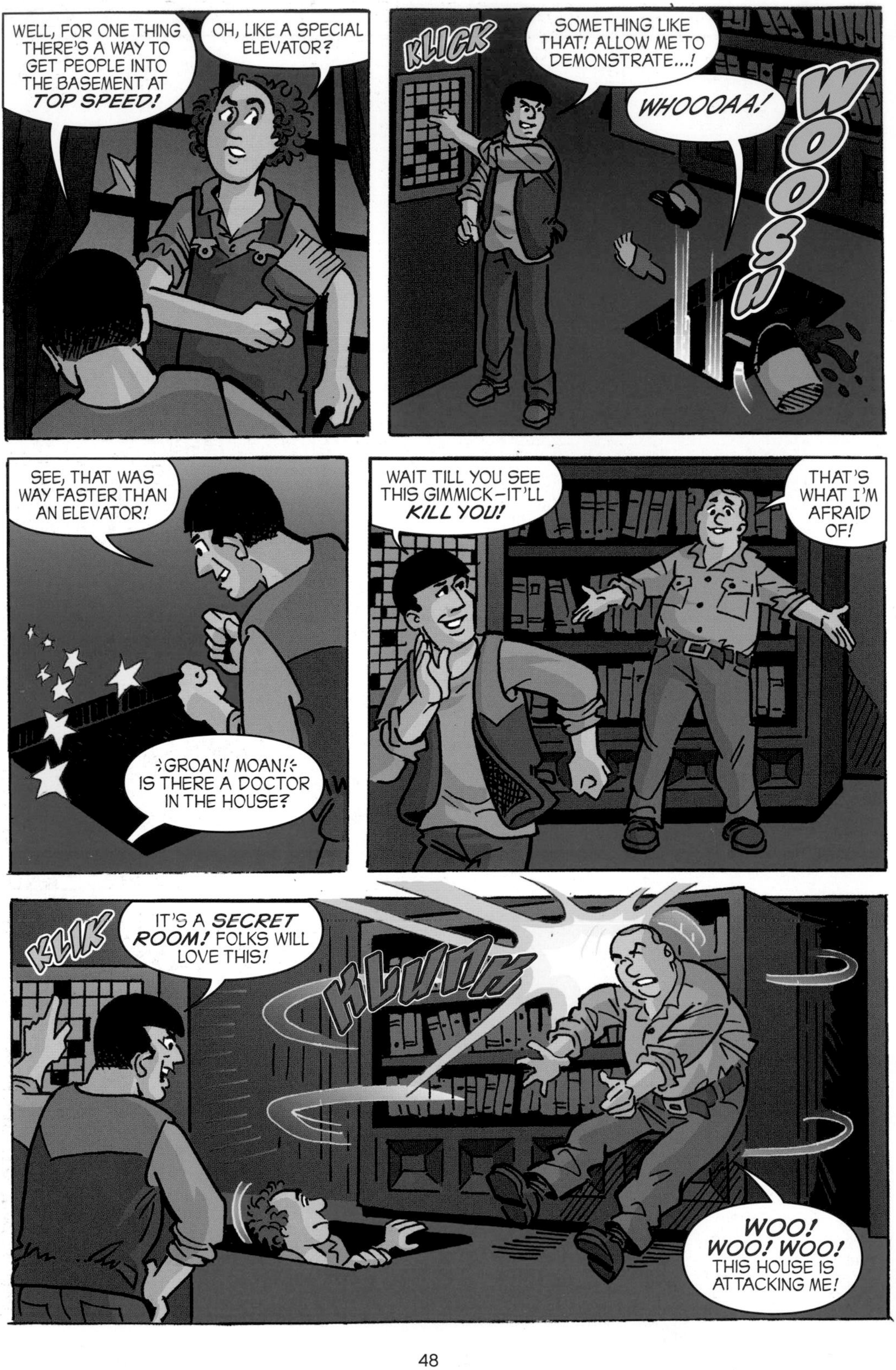
WELL, FOR ONE THING THERE'S A WAY TO GET PEOPLE INTO THE BASEMENT AT TOP SPEED!
OH, LIKE A SPECIAL ELEVATOR?
KLICK
SOMETHING LIKE THAT! ALLOW ME TO DEMONSTRATE...!
WHOOOAA!
WOOSH
SEE, THAT WAS WAY FASTER THAN AN ELEVATOR!
GROAN! MOAN! IS THERE A DOCTOR IN THE HOUSE?
WAIT TILL YOU SEE THIS GIMMICK—IT'LL KILL YOU!
THAT'S WHAT I'M AFRAID OF!
KLIK
IT'S A SECRET ROOM! FOLKS WILL LOVE THIS!
KLUNK
WOO! WOO! WOO! THIS HOUSE IS ATTACKING ME!

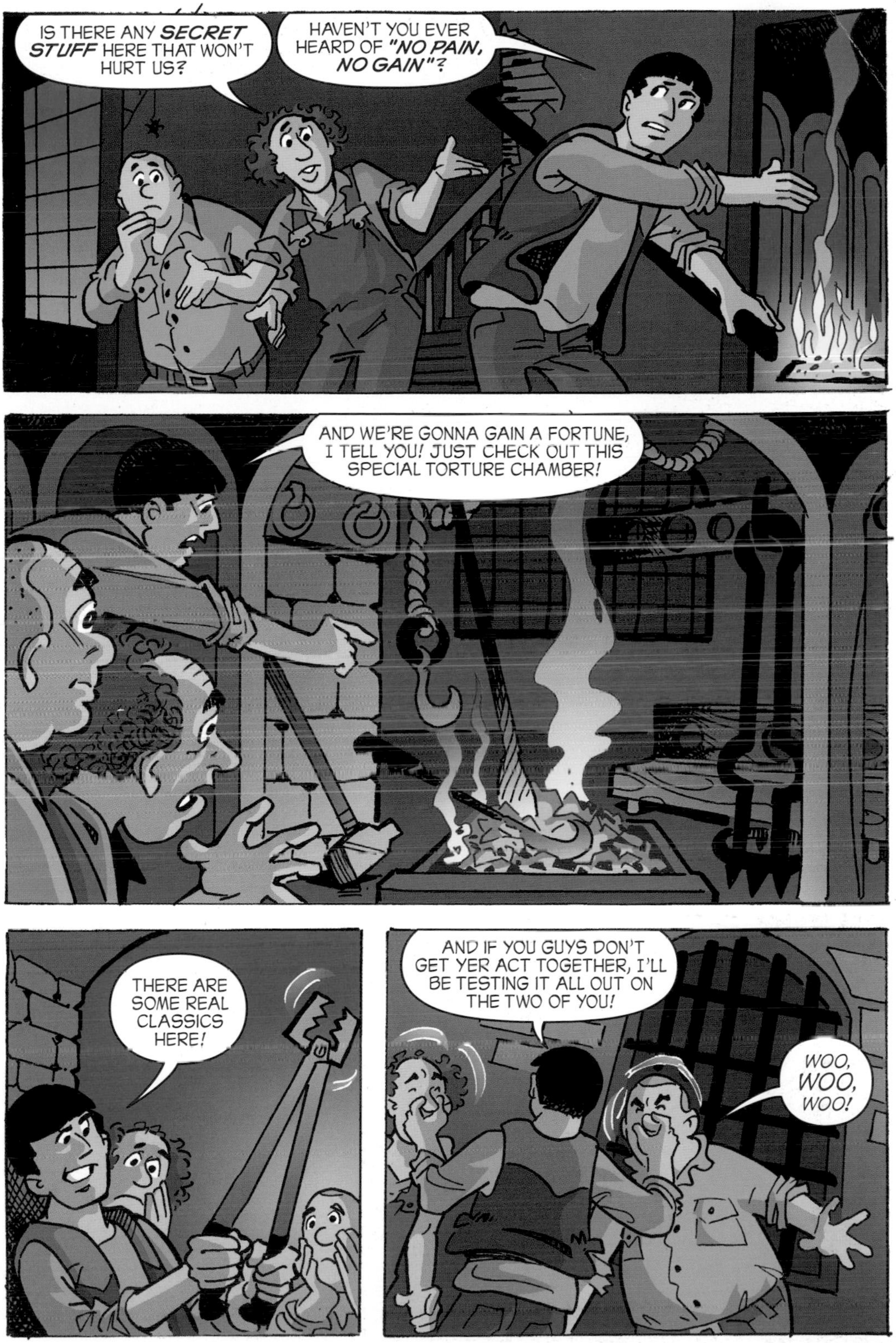

IS THERE ANY **SECRET STUFF** HERE THAT WON'T HURT US?
HAVEN'T YOU EVER HEARD OF ***"NO PAIN, NO GAIN"***?
AND WE'RE GONNA GAIN A FORTUNE, I TELL YOU! JUST CHECK OUT THIS SPECIAL TORTURE CHAMBER!
THERE ARE SOME REAL CLASSICS HERE!
AND IF YOU GUYS DON'T GET YER ACT TOGETHER, I'LL BE TESTING IT ALL OUT ON THE TWO OF YOU!
WOO, WOO, WOO!

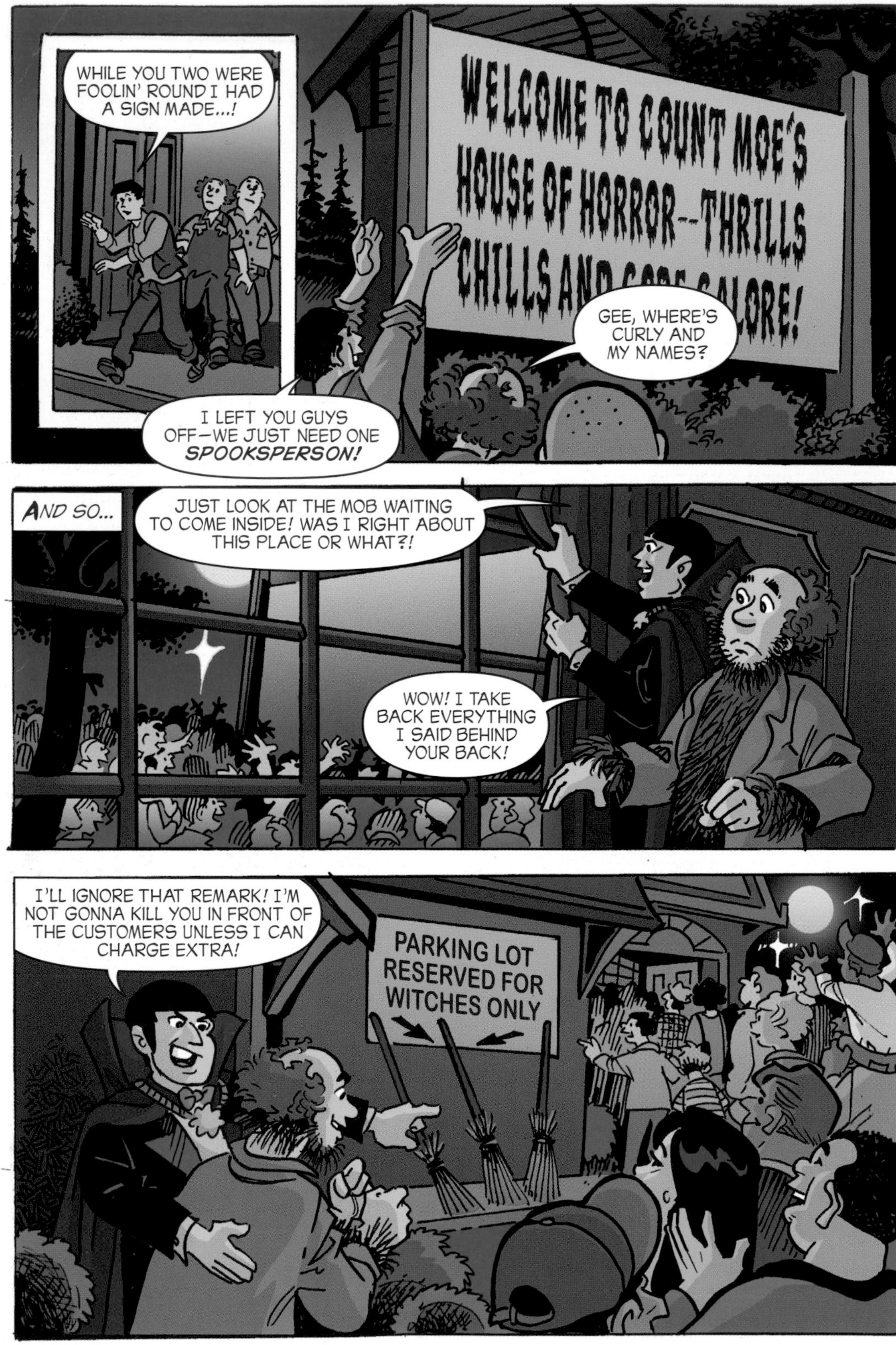
WELCOME TO COUNT MOE'S HOUSE OF HORROR--THRILLS CHILLS AND GORE GALORE!
WHILE YOU TWO WERE FOOLIN' ROUND I HAD A SIGN MADE...!
GEE, WHERE'S CURLY AND MY NAMES?
I LEFT YOU GUYS OFF—WE JUST NEED ONE SPOOKSPERSON!
AND SO...
JUST LOOK AT THE MOB WAITING TO COME INSIDE! WAS I RIGHT ABOUT THIS PLACE OR WHAT?!
WOW! I TAKE BACK EVERYTHING I SAID BEHIND YOUR BACK!
I'LL IGNORE THAT REMARK! I'M NOT GONNA KILL YOU IN FRONT OF THE CUSTOMERS UNLESS I CAN CHARGE EXTRA!
PARKING LOT RESERVED FOR WITCHES ONLY

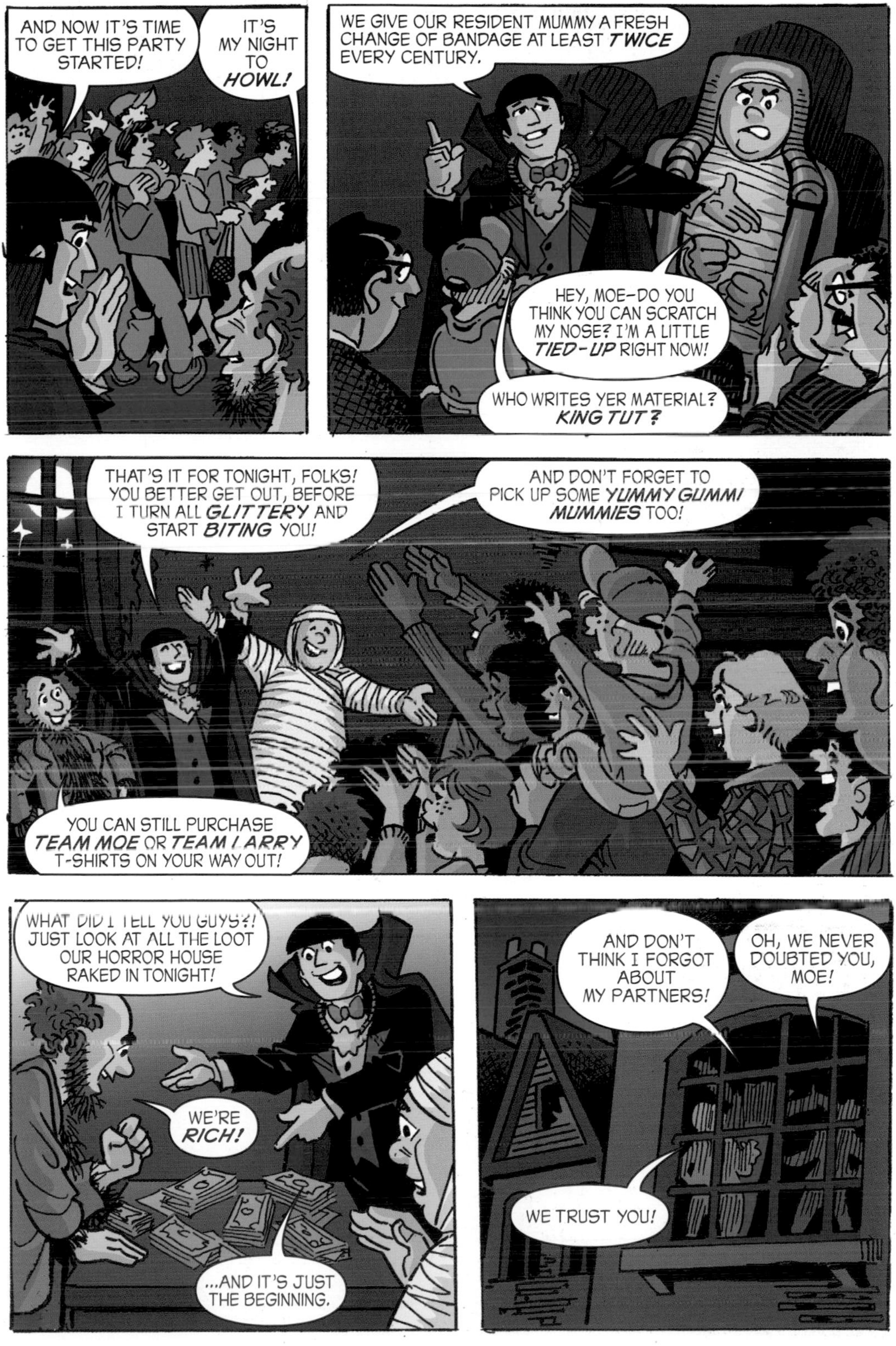
AND NOW IT'S TIME TO GET THIS PARTY STARTED!
IT'S MY NIGHT TO HOWL!
WE GIVE OUR RESIDENT MUMMY A FRESH CHANGE OF BANDAGE AT LEAST TWICE EVERY CENTURY.
HEY, MOE—DO YOU THINK YOU CAN SCRATCH MY NOSE? I'M A LITTLE TIED-UP RIGHT NOW!
WHO WRITES YER MATERIAL? KING TUT?
THAT'S IT FOR TONIGHT, FOLKS! YOU BETTER GET OUT, BEFORE I TURN ALL GLITTERY AND START BITING YOU!
AND DON'T FORGET TO PICK UP SOME YUMMY GUMMI MUMMIES TOO!
YOU CAN STILL PURCHASE TEAM MOE OR TEAM LARRY T-SHIRTS ON YOUR WAY OUT!
WHAT DID I TELL YOU GUYS?! JUST LOOK AT ALL THE LOOT OUR HORROR HOUSE RAKED IN TONIGHT!
WE'RE RICH!
...AND IT'S JUST THE BEGINNING.
AND DON'T THINK I FORGOT ABOUT MY PARTNERS!
OH, WE NEVER DOUBTED YOU, MOE!
WE TRUST YOU!

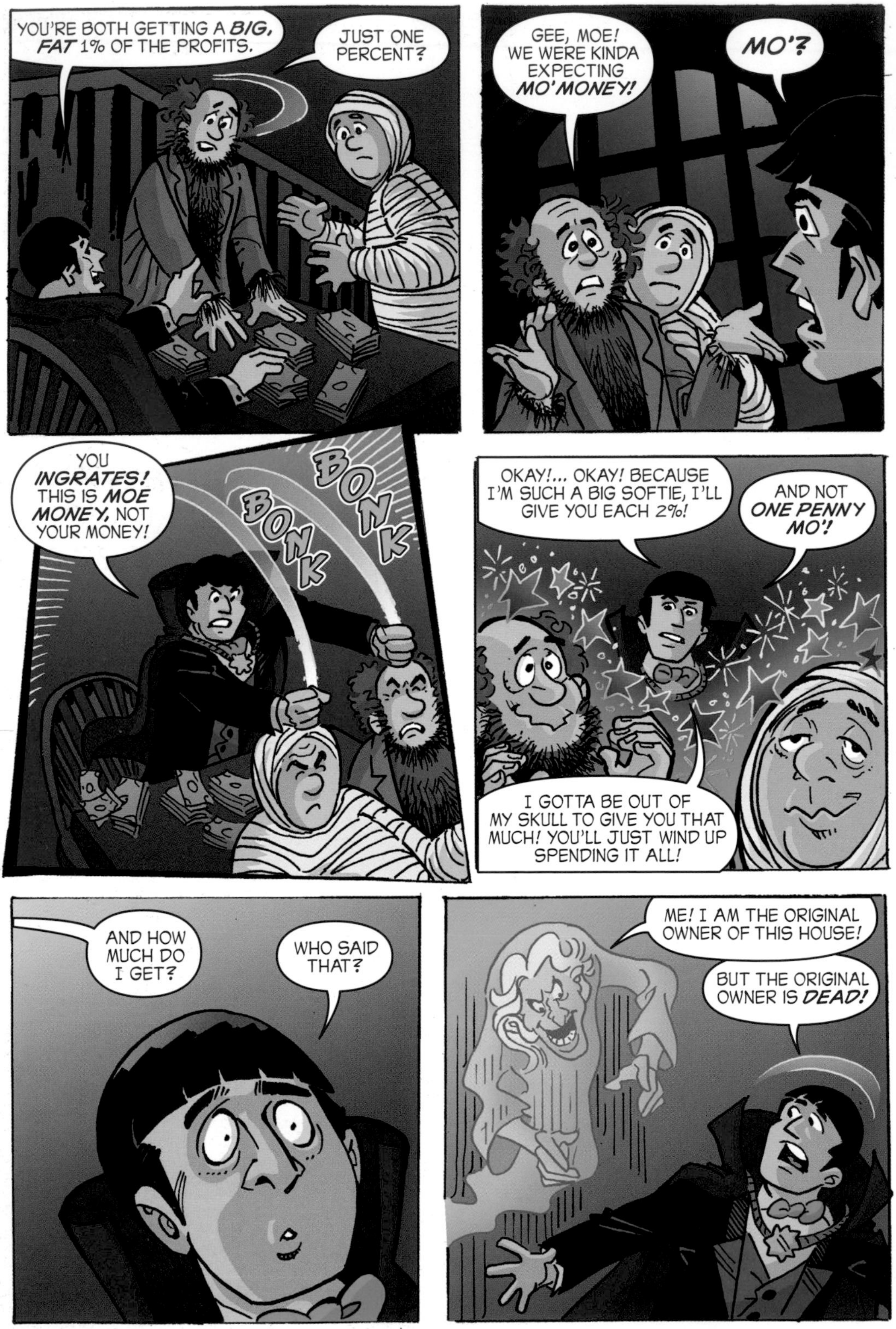
YOU'RE BOTH GETTING A *BIG, FAT* 1% OF THE PROFITS.
JUST ONE PERCENT?
GEE, MOE! WE WERE KINDA EXPECTING *MO' MONEY!*
MO'?
YOU *INGRATES!* THIS IS *MOE MONEY,* NOT YOUR MONEY!
BONK
BONK
OKAY!... OKAY! BECAUSE I'M SUCH A BIG SOFTIE, I'LL GIVE YOU EACH *2%!*
AND NOT *ONE PENNY MO'!*
I GOTTA BE OUT OF MY SKULL TO GIVE YOU THAT MUCH! YOU'LL JUST WIND UP SPENDING IT ALL!
AND HOW MUCH DO I GET?
WHO SAID THAT?
ME! I AM THE ORIGINAL OWNER OF THIS HOUSE!
BUT THE ORIGINAL OWNER IS *DEAD!*

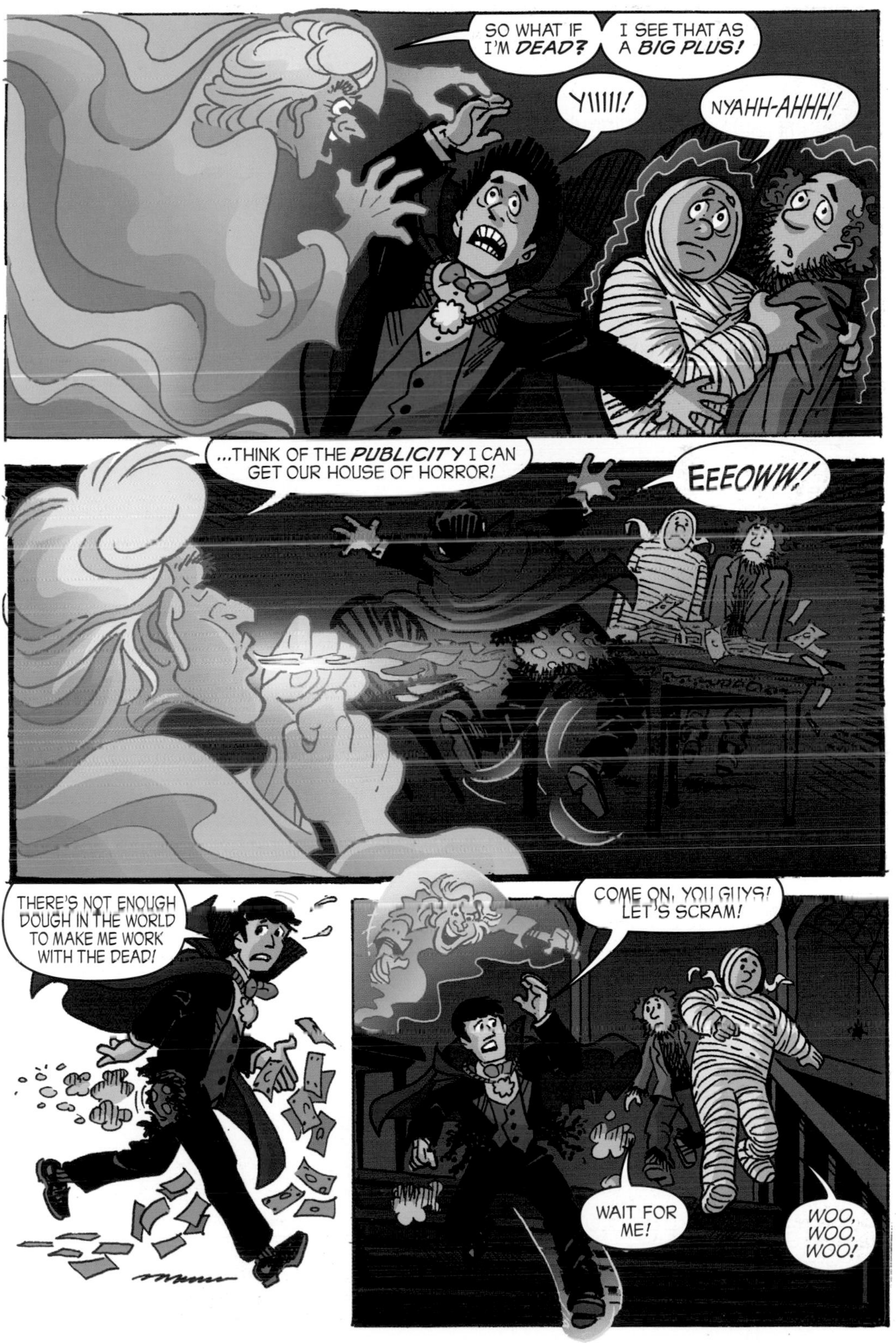
SO WHAT IF I'M *DEAD?*
I SEE THAT AS A *BIG PLUS!*
YIIIII!
NYAHH-AHHH!
...THINK OF THE *PUBLICITY* I CAN GET OUR HOUSE OF HORROR!
EEEOWW!
THERE'S NOT ENOUGH DOUGH IN THE WORLD TO MAKE ME WORK WITH THE DEAD!
COME ON, YOU GUYS! LET'S SCRAM!
WAIT FOR ME!
WOO, WOO, WOO!

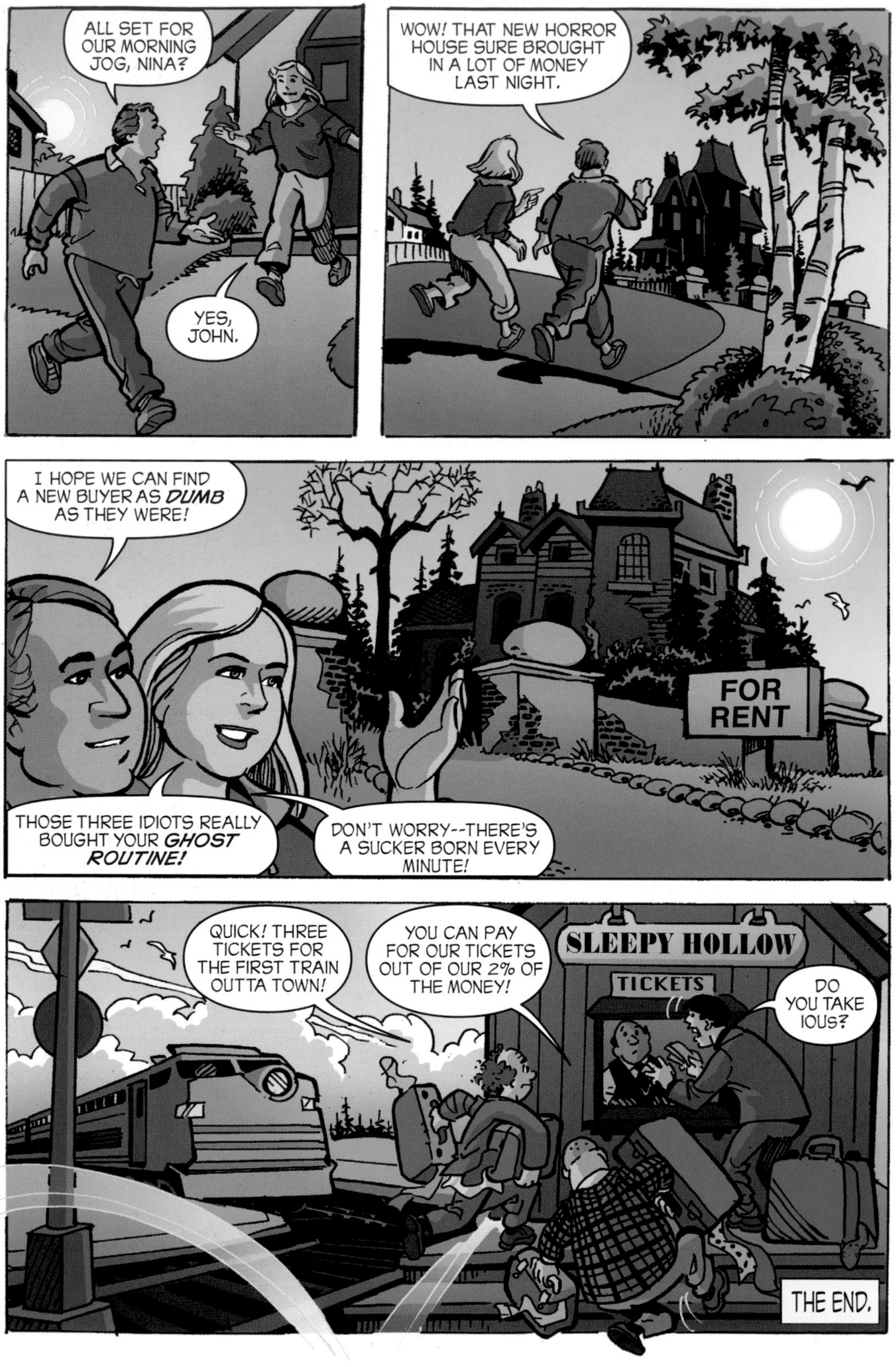
ALL SET FOR OUR MORNING JOG, NINA?
YES, JOHN.
WOW! THAT NEW HORROR HOUSE SURE BROUGHT IN A LOT OF MONEY LAST NIGHT.
I HOPE WE CAN FIND A NEW BUYER AS DUMB AS THEY WERE!
FOR RENT
THOSE THREE IDIOTS REALLY BOUGHT YOUR GHOST ROUTINE!
DON'T WORRY--THERE'S A SUCKER BORN EVERY MINUTE!
SLEEPY HOLLOW
TICKETS
QUICK! THREE TICKETS FOR THE FIRST TRAIN OUTTA TOWN!
YOU CAN PAY FOR OUR TICKETS OUT OF OUR 2% OF THE MONEY!
DO YOU TAKE IOUS?
THE END.

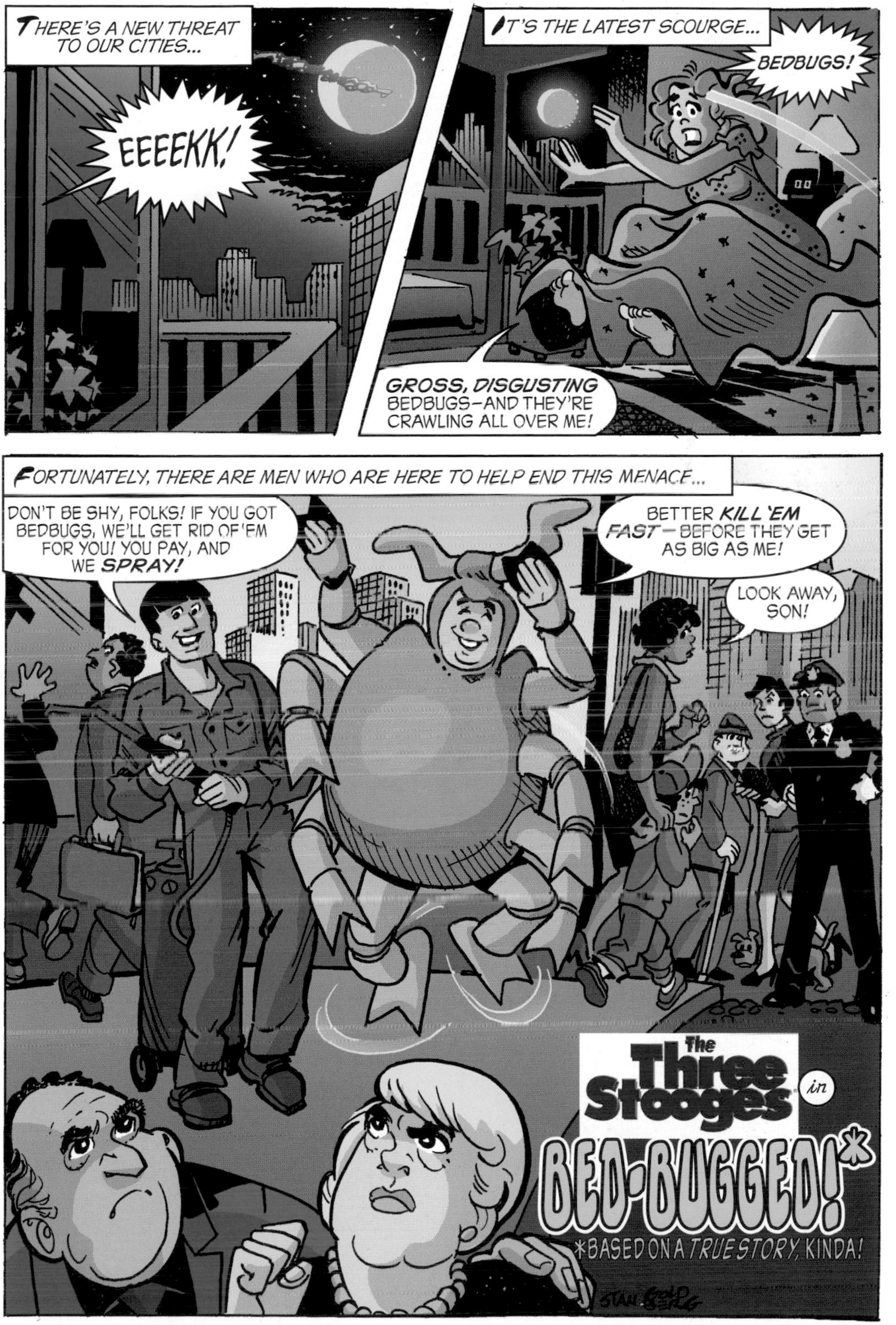

THERE'S A NEW THREAT TO OUR CITIES...
EEEEKK!
IT'S THE LATEST SCOURGE...
BEDBUGS!
GROSS, DISGUSTING BEDBUGS—AND THEY'RE CRAWLING ALL OVER ME!
FORTUNATELY, THERE ARE MEN WHO ARE HERE TO HELP END THIS MENACE...
DON'T BE SHY, FOLKS! IF YOU GOT BEDBUGS, WE'LL GET RID OF 'EM FOR YOU! YOU PAY, AND WE SPRAY!
BETTER KILL 'EM FAST—BEFORE THEY GET AS BIG AS ME!
LOOK AWAY, SON!
The Three Stooges in
BED-BUGGED!*
*BASED ON A TRUE STORY, KINDA!

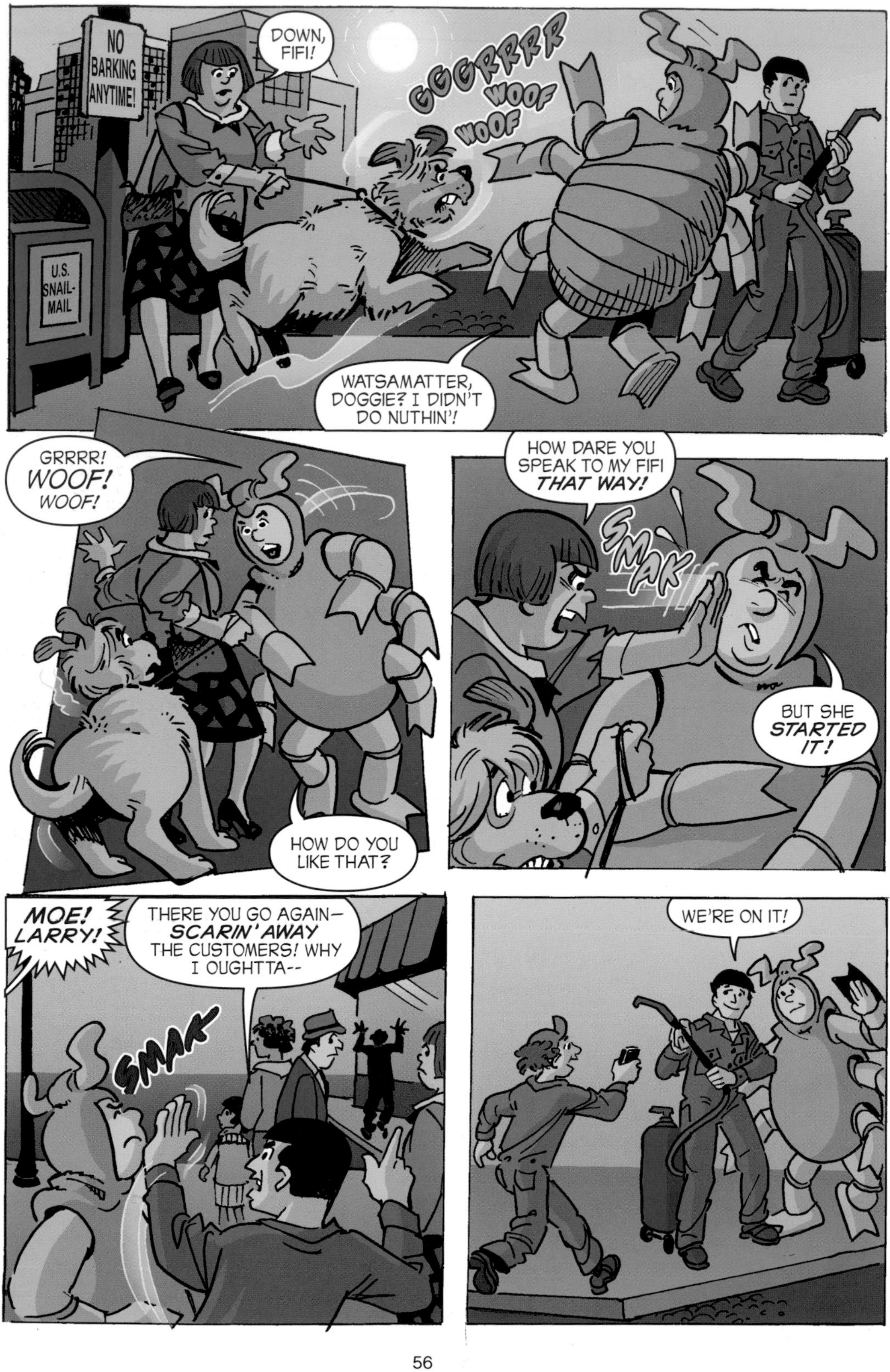
NO BARKING ANYTIME!
DOWN, FIFI!
GGGRRRR WOOF WOOF
U.S. SNAIL-MAIL
WATSAMATTER, DOGGIE? I DIDN'T DO NUTHIN'!
GRRRR! WOOF! WOOF!
HOW DO YOU LIKE THAT?
HOW DARE YOU SPEAK TO MY FIFI THAT WAY!
SMAK
BUT SHE STARTED IT!
MOE! LARRY!
THERE YOU GO AGAIN— SCARIN' AWAY THE CUSTOMERS! WHY I OUGHTTA--
SMAK
WE'RE ON IT!

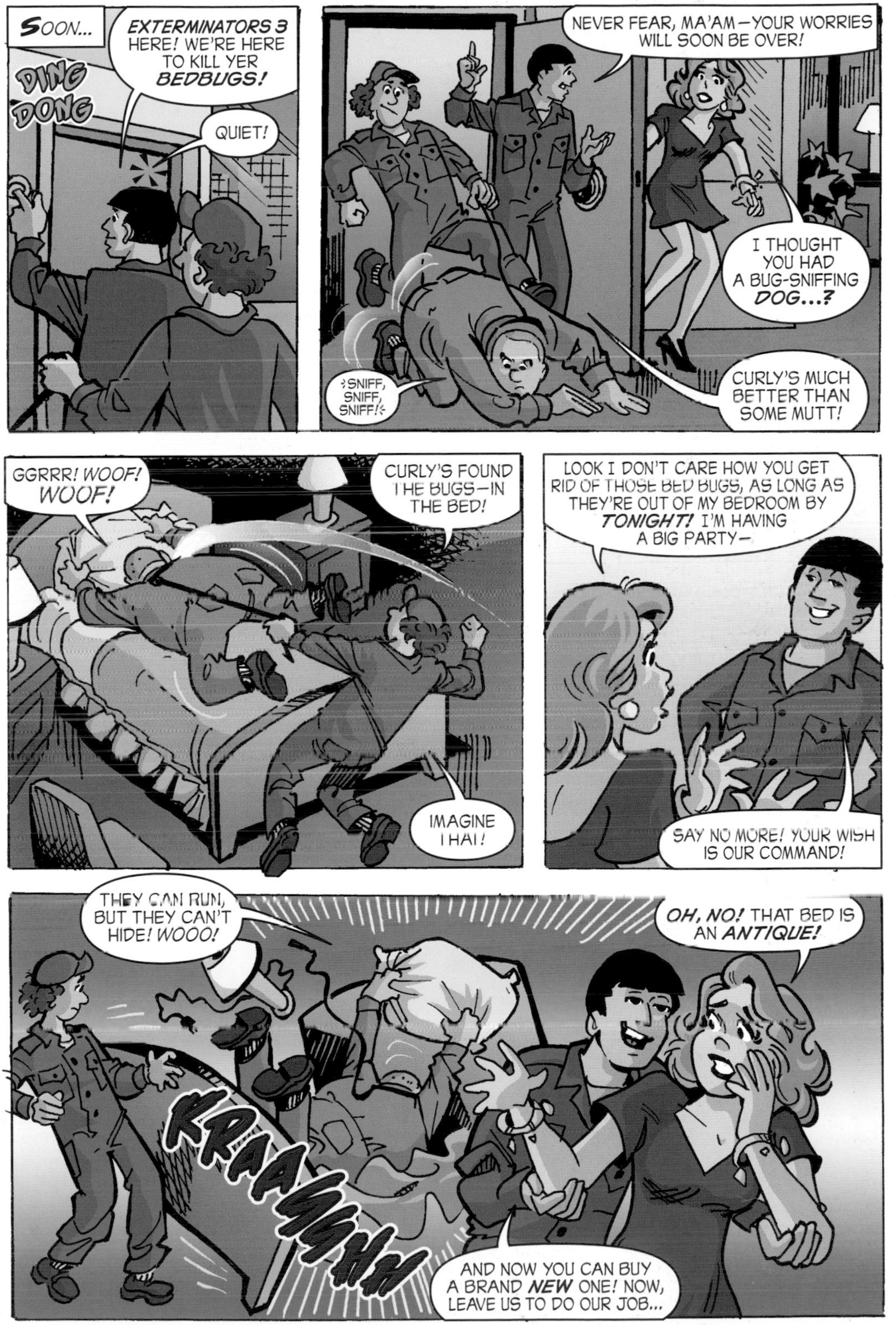

SOON...
EXTERMINATORS 3 HERE! WE'RE HERE TO KILL YER BEDBUGS!
DING DONG
QUIET!
NEVER FEAR, MA'AM—YOUR WORRIES WILL SOON BE OVER!
I THOUGHT YOU HAD A BUG-SNIFFING DOG...?
SNIFF, SNIFF, SNIFF!
CURLY'S MUCH BETTER THAN SOME MUTT!
GGRRR! WOOF! WOOF!
CURLY'S FOUND THE BUGS—IN THE BED!
IMAGINE THAT!
LOOK I DON'T CARE HOW YOU GET RID OF THOSE BED BUGS, AS LONG AS THEY'RE OUT OF MY BEDROOM BY TONIGHT! I'M HAVING A BIG PARTY—
SAY NO MORE! YOUR WISH IS OUR COMMAND!
THEY CAN RUN, BUT THEY CAN'T HIDE! WOOO!
OH, NO! THAT BED IS AN ANTIQUE!
KRAAASHH
AND NOW YOU CAN BUY A BRAND NEW ONE! NOW, LEAVE US TO DO OUR JOB...

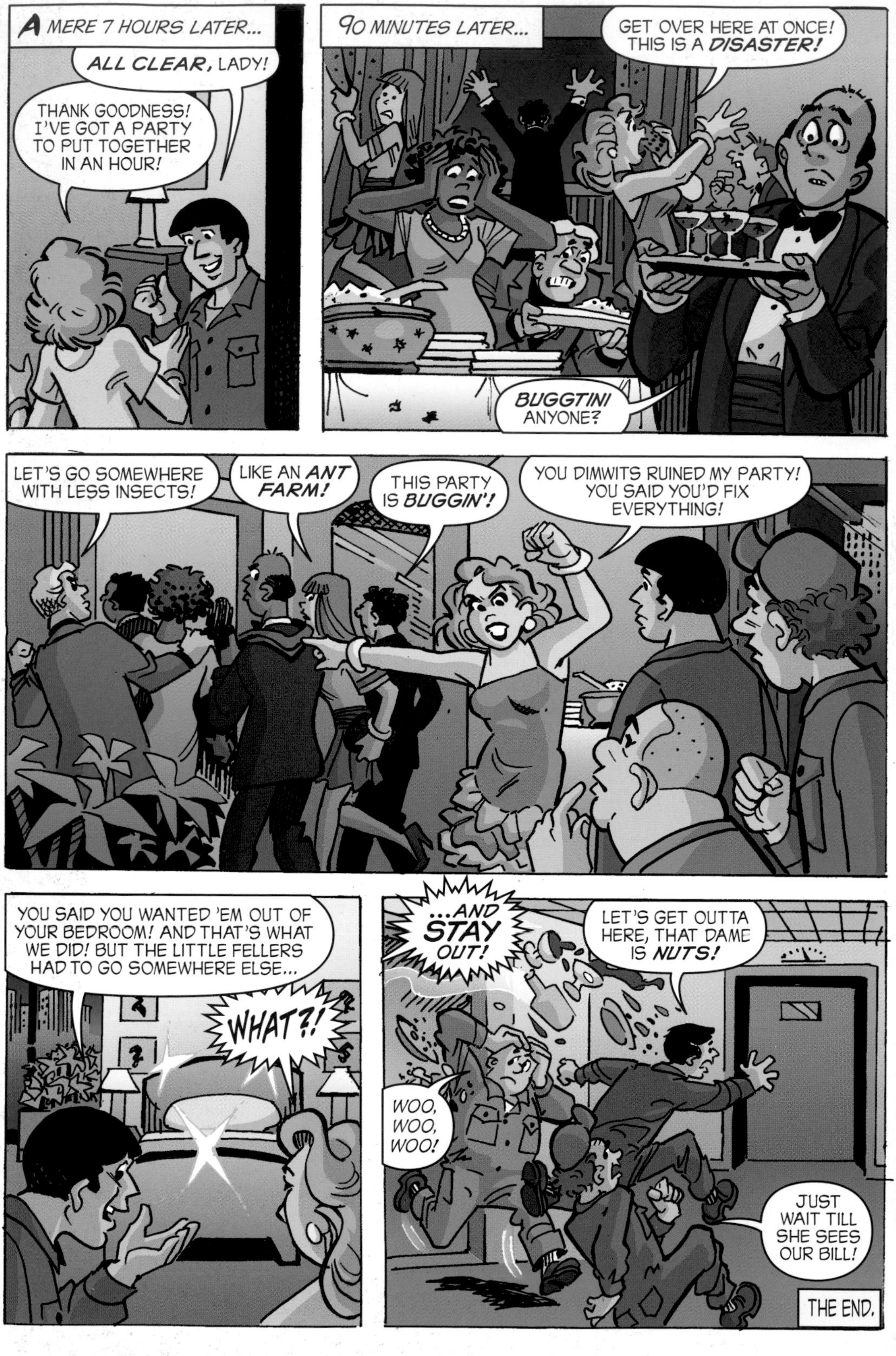
A MERE 7 HOURS LATER...
ALL CLEAR, LADY!
THANK GOODNESS! I'VE GOT A PARTY TO PUT TOGETHER IN AN HOUR!
90 MINUTES LATER...
GET OVER HERE AT ONCE! THIS IS A DISASTER!
BUGGTINI ANYONE?
LET'S GO SOMEWHERE WITH LESS INSECTS!
LIKE AN ANT FARM!
THIS PARTY IS BUGGIN'!
YOU DIMWITS RUINED MY PARTY! YOU SAID YOU'D FIX EVERYTHING!
YOU SAID YOU WANTED 'EM OUT OF YOUR BEDROOM! AND THAT'S WHAT WE DID! BUT THE LITTLE FELLERS HAD TO GO SOMEWHERE ELSE...
WHAT?!
...AND STAY OUT!
LET'S GET OUTTA HERE, THAT DAME IS NUTS!
WOO, WOO, WOO!
JUST WAIT TILL SHE SEES OUR BILL!
THE END.

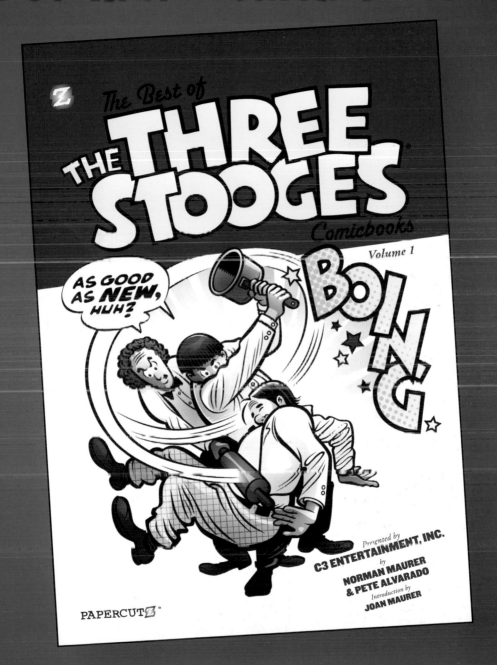

WATCH OUT FOR PAPERCUTZ™

Welcome to the premiere THREE STOOGES graphic novel from Papercutz, the folks dedicated to creating great graphic novels for all ages. I'm Jim Salicrup, the Editor-in-Chief and Ted Healy-type of this outfit.

This certainly isn't the first time THE THREE STOOGES have been in comics. Way back when, the comicbook adventures of the Stooges were written and illustrated by the incredibly talented Norman Maurer, who actually wound up married to Moe's daughter Joan. Norman eventually went on to be involved in the production of many of the Three Stooges movies. Another acclaimed comicbook artist and animator, Peter Alvarado, illustrated many a THREE STOOGES comicbook as well, and Papercutz is proud to offer up samples of their work in THE BEST OF THE THREE STOOGES COMICBOOKS, a hardcover collection of these classic old funny books that's available now at booksellers everywhere. The book is like finding a treasure trove of a bunch of old, well-worn comics that you'll want to savor for years to come. Check out the excerpt on the following pages.

But just as the Stooges have miraculously returned to the big screen, they've also returned to comics pages, thanks to a couple of major comicbook legends—George Gladir and Stan Goldberg.

George began writing back in 1959 for Archie Comics and wrote such titles as ARCHIE'S JOKEBOOK, ARCHIE'S GALS BETTY AND VERONICA, ARCHIE'S PAL JUGHEAD, REGGIE AND ME, BETTY AND ME, and my favorite, ARCHIE'S MADHOUSE, where he created, with artist Dan DeCarlo, Sabrina the Teen-Age Witch! If that wasn't enough he was also the head writer for thirty years for CRACKED magazine, and more recently George collaborated with Stan Golberg on the comic CINDY AND HER OBASAN. In 2007, George won the Bill Finger Award for Excellence in Comic Book Writing.

Stan Goldberg, at age 16, began working as a colorist at the company that would become Marvel Comics. Stan was the color designer for such famous characters as Spider-Man, The Fantastic Four, the X-Men, and the Incredible Hulk. Stan began drawing comics as well, illustrating tales of horror, romance, funny animals, and such titles as PATSY WALKER, MY GIRL PATSY, and MILLIE THE MODEL. Stan also worked for DC Comics on their teen-titles, such as DEBBY, BINKY, and SCOOTER. Eventually, Stan began a long relationship with Archie Comics, drawing just about all of their titles at one time or another, as well as the syndicated Archie Sunday newspaper comic strip. Stan also drew the surprising crossover between Marvel's vengeful vigilante and Archie's gang from Riverdale in the unforgettable ARCHIE MEETS THE PUNISHER. More recently Stan illustrated the best-selling ARCHIE GETS MARRIED, written by famed Batman Executive Producer Michael Uslan.

As Editor-in-Chief, and sometime comicbook writer, and fan of the Three Stooges, I couldn't resist the chance to write a story that Stan would illustrate, and the result is "Bed-Bugged!" I also couldn't resist adding a few jokes and puns to George's scripts, so if there's any bits in George's stories that aren't as good as the rest—you can blame me for dragging the quality down!

There's a lot more I wanted to say about the Stooges themselves, but just including these super-mini career biographies of George and Stan has taken up all the space I have, so I'll have to wait for THE THREE STOOGES #2 "Ebenezer Stooge" to continue on.

JIM

Special preview of THE BEST OF THE THREE STOOGES COMICBOOKS Vol. 1…

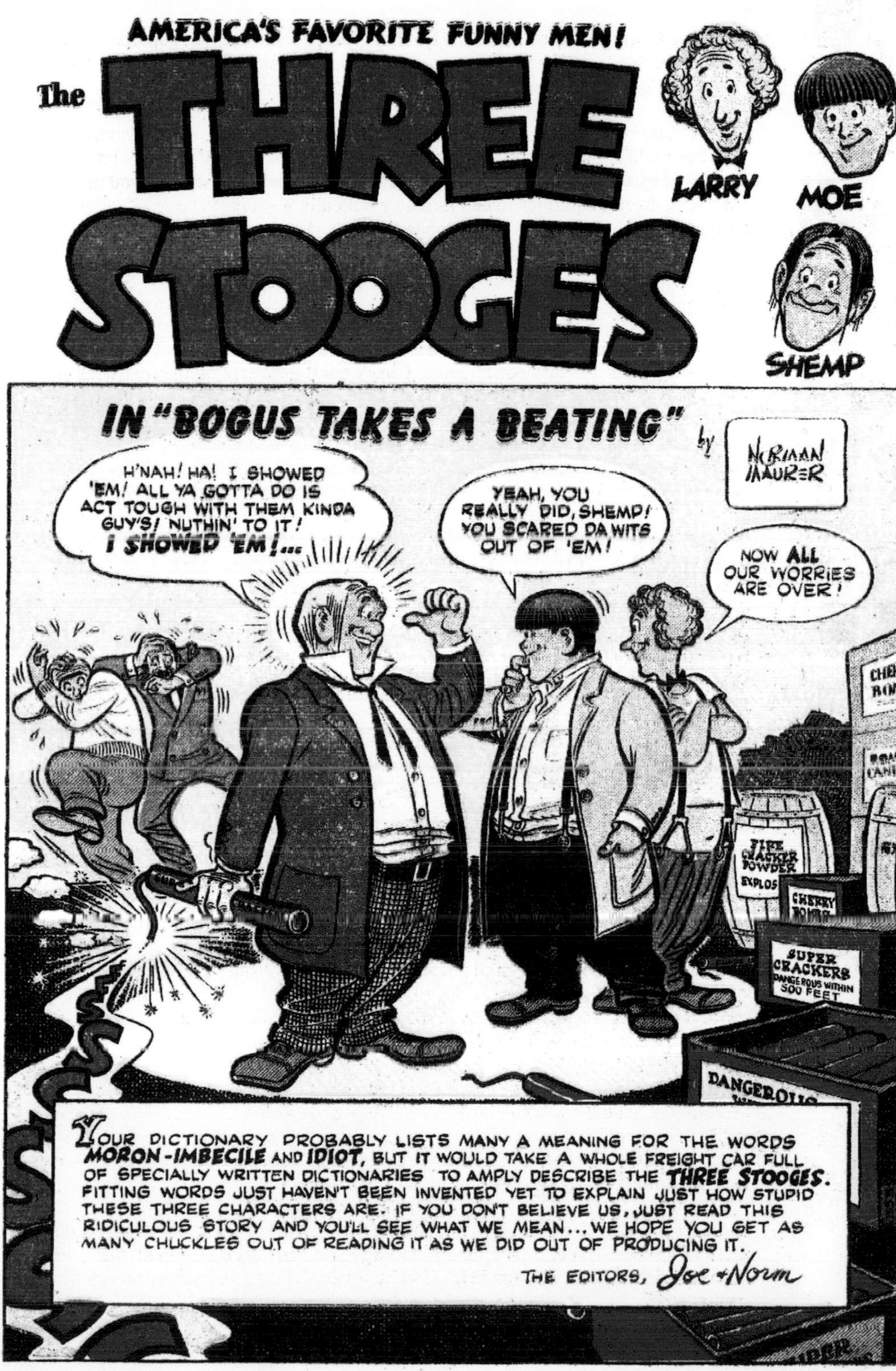
AMERICA'S FAVORITE FUNNY MEN!
The THREE STOOGES
LARRY
MOE
SHEMP
IN "BOGUS TAKES A BEATING"
by NORMAN MAURER
H'NAH! HA! I SHOWED 'EM! ALL YA GOTTA DO IS ACT TOUGH WITH THEM KINDA GUY'S! NUTHIN' TO IT! I SHOWED 'EM!...
YEAH, YOU REALLY DID, SHEMP! YOU SCARED DA WITS OUT OF 'EM!
NOW ALL OUR WORRIES ARE OVER!
FIRE CRACKER POWDER
SUPER CRACKERS DANGEROUS WITHIN 500 FEET
YOUR DICTIONARY PROBABLY LISTS MANY A MEANING FOR THE WORDS MORON-IMBECILE AND IDIOT, BUT IT WOULD TAKE A WHOLE FREIGHT CAR FULL OF SPECIALLY WRITTEN DICTIONARIES TO AMPLY DESCRIBE THE THREE STOOGES. FITTING WORDS JUST HAVEN'T BEEN INVENTED YET TO EXPLAIN JUST HOW STUPID THESE THREE CHARACTERS ARE. IF YOU DON'T BELIEVE US, JUST READ THIS RIDICULOUS STORY AND YOU'LL SEE WHAT WE MEAN... WE HOPE YOU GET AS MANY CHUCKLES OUT OF READING IT AS WE DID OUT OF PRODUCING IT.
THE EDITORS, Joe + Norm

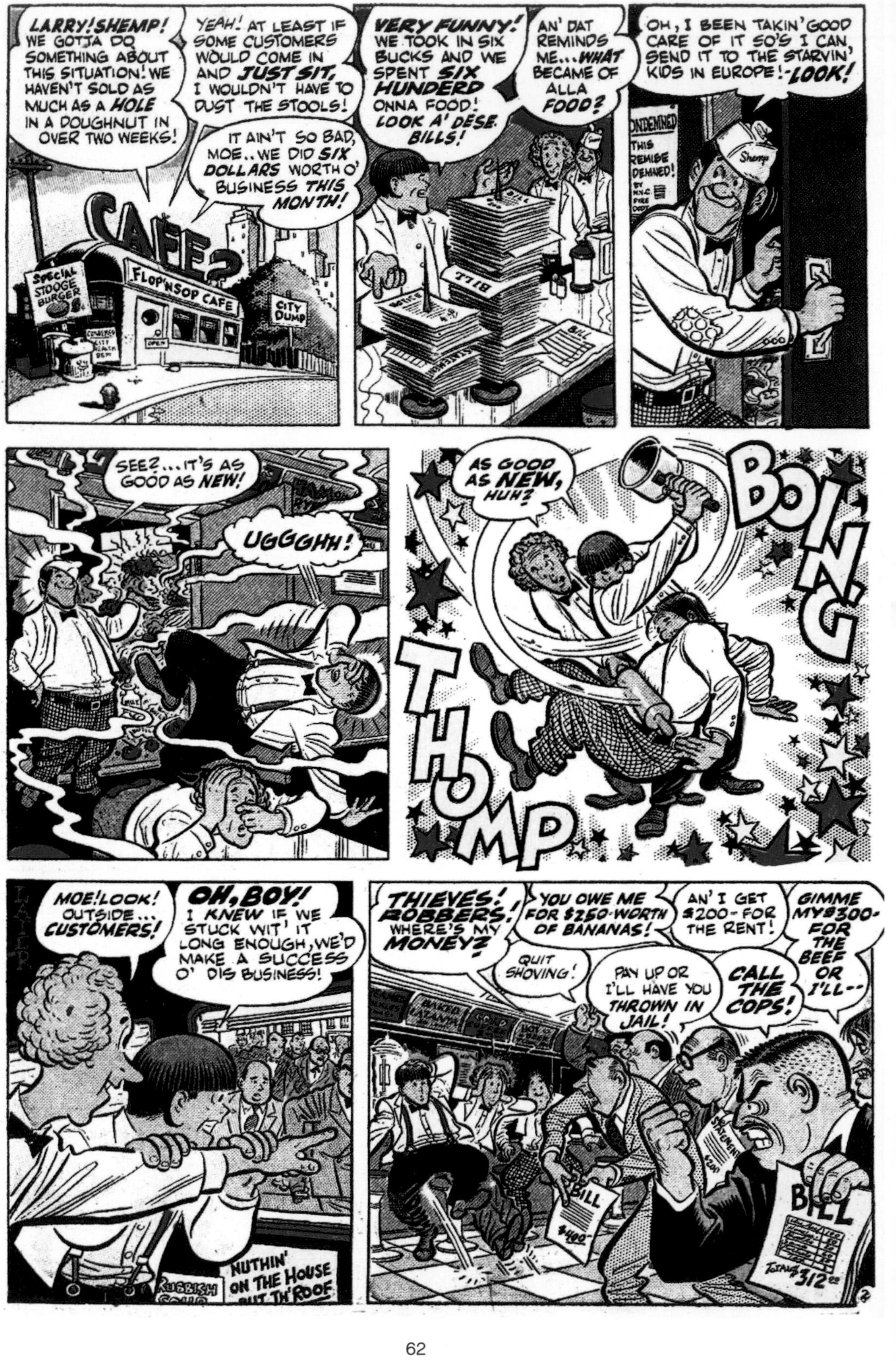
LARRY! SHEMP! WE GOTTA DO SOMETHING ABOUT THIS SITUATION! WE HAVEN'T SOLD AS MUCH AS A HOLE IN A DOUGHNUT IN OVER TWO WEEKS!
YEAH! AT LEAST IF SOME CUSTOMERS WOULD COME IN AND JUST SIT, I WOULDN'T HAVE TO DUST THE STOOLS!
IT AIN'T SO BAD, MOE.. WE DID SIX DOLLARS WORTH O' BUSINESS THIS MONTH!
CAFE?
SPECIAL STOOGE BURGER
FLOP'N SOP CAFE
CITY DUMP
OPEN
VERY FUNNY! WE TOOK IN SIX BUCKS AND WE SPENT SIX HUNDERD ONNA FOOD! LOOK A' DESE BILLS!
BILL
AN' DAT REMINDS ME... WHAT BECAME OF ALLA FOOD?
OH, I BEEN TAKIN' GOOD CARE OF IT SO'S I CAN SEND IT TO THE STARVIN' KIDS IN EUROPE! -LOOK!
Shemp
SEE?... IT'S AS GOOD AS NEW!
UGGGHH!
AS GOOD AS NEW, HUH?
BOING
THOMP
MOE! LOOK! OUTSIDE... CUSTOMERS!
OH, BOY! I KNEW IF WE STUCK WIT' IT LONG ENOUGH, WE'D MAKE A SUCCESS O' DIS BUSINESS!
LATER
NUTHIN' ON THE HOUSE BUT TH' ROOF
RUBBISH SOUP
THIEVES! ROBBERS! WHERE'S MY MONEY?
YOU OWE ME FOR $250-WORTH OF BANANAS!
AN' I GET $200-FOR THE RENT!
GIMME MY $300-FOR THE BEEF OR I'LL--
QUIT SHOVING!
PAY UP OR I'LL HAVE YOU THROWN IN JAIL!
CALL THE COPS!
BILL
STATEMENT
BILL
2

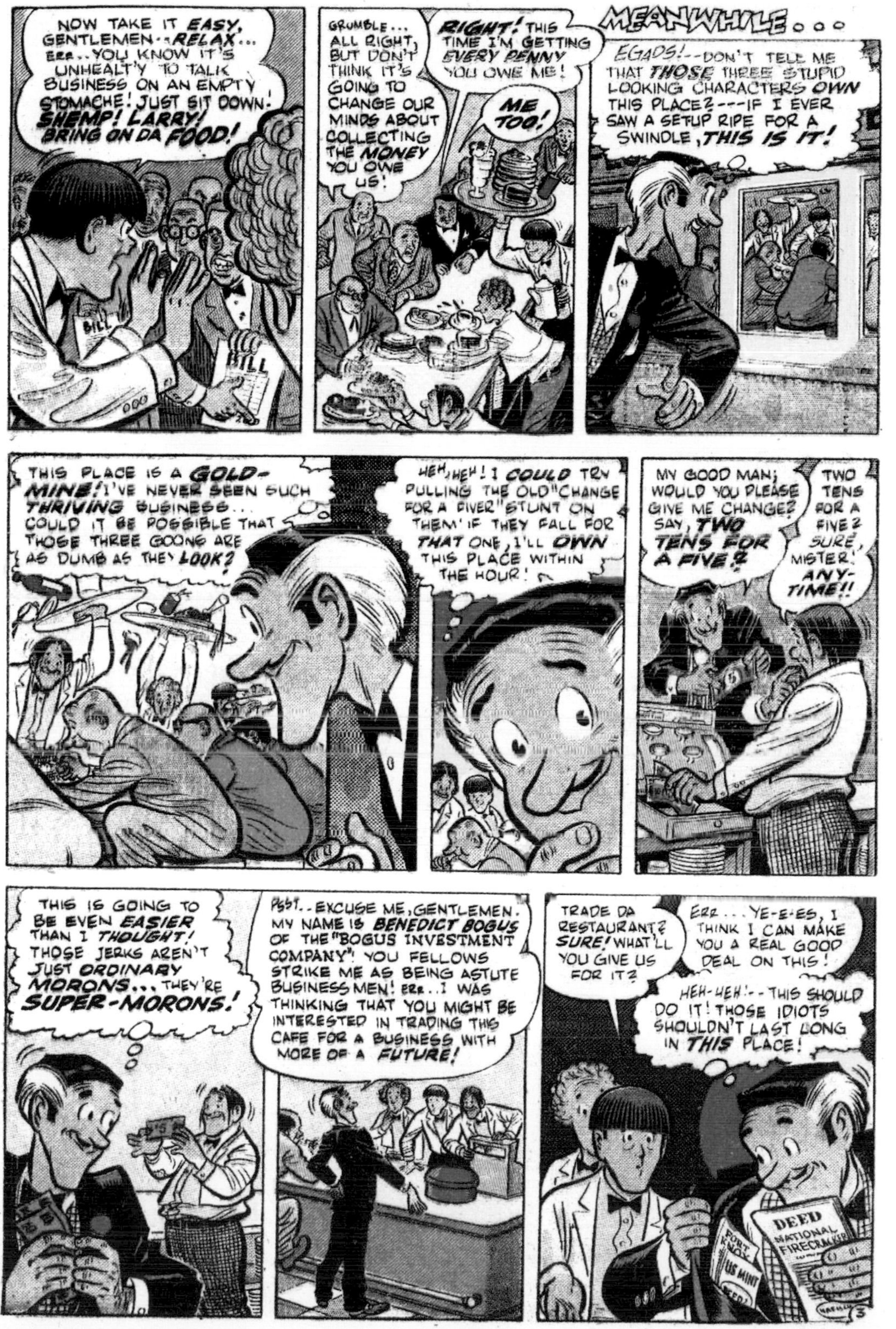

NOW TAKE IT EASY, GENTLEMEN--RELAX... ERR..YOU KNOW IT'S UNHEALT'Y TO TALK BUSINESS ON AN EMPTY STOMACHE! JUST SIT DOWN! SHEMP! LARRY! BRING ON DA FOOD!
BILL
BILL
GRUMBLE... ALL RIGHT, BUT DON'T THINK IT'S GOING TO CHANGE OUR MINDS ABOUT COLLECTING THE MONEY YOU OWE US!
RIGHT! THIS TIME I'M GETTING EVERY PENNY YOU OWE ME!
ME TOO!
MEANWHILE...
EGADS!--DON'T TELL ME THAT THOSE THREE STUPID LOOKING CHARACTERS OWN THIS PLACE?---IF I EVER SAW A SETUP RIPE FOR A SWINDLE, THIS IS IT!
THIS PLACE IS A GOLD-MINE! I'VE NEVER SEEN SUCH THRIVING BUSINESS... COULD IT BE POSSIBLE THAT THOSE THREE GOONS ARE AS DUMB AS THEY LOOK?
HEH, HEH! I COULD TRY PULLING THE OLD "CHANGE FOR A FIVER" STUNT ON THEM! IF THEY FALL FOR THAT ONE, I'LL OWN THIS PLACE WITHIN THE HOUR!
MY GOOD MAN; WOULD YOU PLEASE GIVE ME CHANGE? SAY, TWO TENS FOR A FIVE?
TWO TENS FOR A FIVE? SURE, MISTER! ANY-TIME!!
THIS IS GOING TO BE EVEN EASIER THAN I THOUGHT! THOSE JERKS AREN'T JUST ORDINARY MORONS... THEY'RE SUPER-MORONS!
PSST..EXCUSE ME, GENTLEMEN. MY NAME IS BENEDICT BOGUS OF THE "BOGUS INVESTMENT COMPANY"! YOU FELLOWS STRIKE ME AS BEING ASTUTE BUSINESS MEN! ERR..I WAS THINKING THAT YOU MIGHT BE INTERESTED IN TRADING THIS CAFE FOR A BUSINESS WITH MORE OF A FUTURE!
TRADE DA RESTAURANT? SURE! WHAT'LL YOU GIVE US FOR IT?
ERR... YE-E-ES, I THINK I CAN MAKE YOU A REAL GOOD DEAL ON THIS!
HEH-HEH!--THIS SHOULD DO IT! THOSE IDIOTS SHOULDN'T LAST LONG IN THIS PLACE!
DEED NATIONAL FIRECRACKER
FORT KNOX
US MINT
3

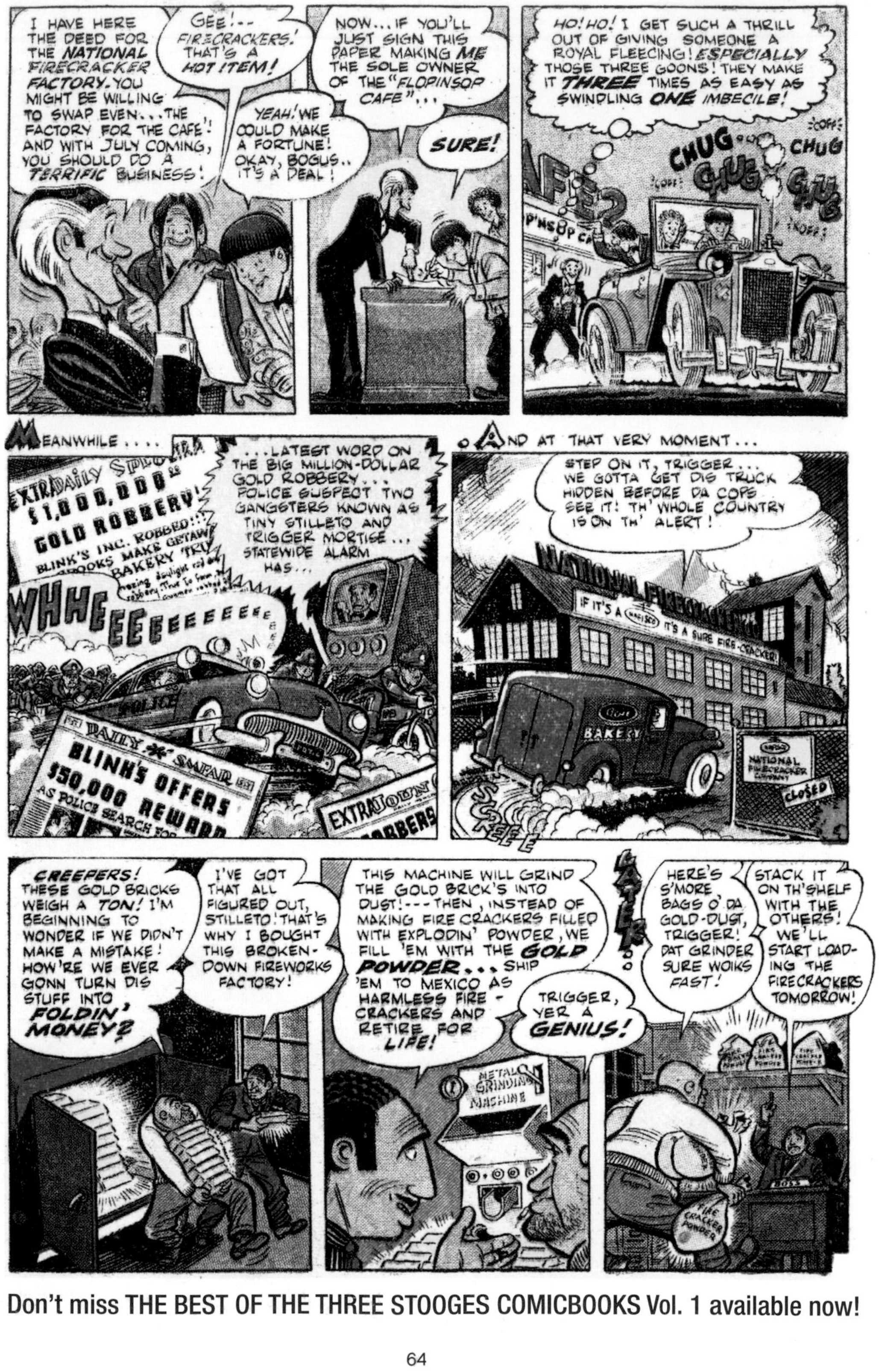

I HAVE HERE THE DEED FOR THE NATIONAL FIRECRACKER FACTORY. YOU MIGHT BE WILLING TO SWAP EVEN... THE FACTORY FOR THE CAFE'! AND WITH JULY COMING, YOU SHOULD DO A TERRIFIC BUSINESS!
GEE!-- FIRECRACKERS! THAT'S A HOT ITEM!
YEAH! WE COULD MAKE A FORTUNE! OKAY, BOGUS.. IT'S A DEAL!
NOW... IF YOU'LL JUST SIGN THIS PAPER MAKING ME THE SOLE OWNER OF THE "FLOPINSOP CAFE"...
SURE!
HO! HO! I GET SUCH A THRILL OUT OF GIVING SOMEONE A ROYAL FLEECING! ESPECIALLY THOSE THREE GOONS! THEY MAKE IT THREE TIMES AS EASY AS SWINDLING ONE IMBECILE!
CHUG CHUG CHUG CHUG
COFF! COFF! KOFF!
MEANWHILE....
$1,000,000 GOLD ROBBERY!
BLINK'S INC. ROBBED
BAKERY
...LATEST WORD ON THE BIG MILLION-DOLLAR GOLD ROBBERY... POLICE SUSPECT TWO GANGSTERS KNOWN AS TINY STILLETO AND TRIGGER MORTISE... STATEWIDE ALARM HAS...
WHHEEEEEEEEEE
POLICE
BLINK'S OFFERS $50,000 REWARD AS POLICE SEARCH FOR
EXTRA
ROBBERS
AND AT THAT VERY MOMENT...
STEP ON IT, TRIGGER... WE GOTTA GET DIS TRUCK HIDDEN BEFORE DA COPS SEE IT! TH' WHOLE COUNTRY IS ON TH' ALERT!
NATIONAL FIRECRACKER CO.
IF IT'S A NAFISCO IT'S A SURE FIRE-CRACKER!
BAKERY
NATIONAL FIRECRACKER COMPANY
CLOSED
SCREEEE
CREEPERS! THESE GOLD BRICKS WEIGH A TON! I'M BEGINNING TO WONDER IF WE DIDN'T MAKE A MISTAKE! HOW'RE WE EVER GONN TURN DIS STUFF INTO FOLDIN' MONEY?
I'VE GOT THAT ALL FIGURED OUT, STILLETO! THAT'S WHY I BOUGHT THIS BROKEN-DOWN FIREWORKS FACTORY!
THIS MACHINE WILL GRIND THE GOLD BRICK'S INTO DUST!---THEN, INSTEAD OF MAKING FIRE CRACKERS FILLED WITH EXPLODIN' POWDER, WE FILL 'EM WITH THE GOLD POWDER... SHIP 'EM TO MEXICO AS HARMLESS FIRE-CRACKERS AND RETIRE FOR LIFE!
TRIGGER, YER A GENIUS!
METAL GRINDING MACHINE
HERE'S S'MORE BAGS O' DA GOLD-DUST, TRIGGER! DAT GRINDER SURE WOIKS FAST!
STACK IT ON TH'SHELF WITH THE OTHERS! WE'LL START LOADING THE FIRECRACKERS TOMORROW!
FIRE CRACKER POWDER
BOSS

Don't miss THE BEST OF THE THREE STOOGES COMICBOOKS Vol. 1 available now!